After Elaine

After Elaine

Ann L. Dreyer

Cricket Books
Chicago

—For my mom and dad,
who always encouraged me to write.

Printed in the United States of America
Designed by Anthony Jacobson
First edition, 2002

Library of Congress Cataloging-in-Publication Data

Dreyer, Ann L.
After Elaine / Ann L. Dreyer.
p. cm.
Summary: Gina relives events that preceded her angry, hostile, older sister Elaine's senseless death, as her family struggles with their grief and Gina faces the added pressures of starting middle school.
ISBN 0-8126-2651-6 (Cloth : alk. paper)
[1. Sisters—Fiction. 2. Death—Fiction. 3. Schools—Fiction. 4. Family problems—Fiction.] I. Title.
PZ7.D78396 Af 2002
[Fic]—dc21

2002000593

After Elaine

Foreword

THE BARE WALLS OF THE DETENTION ROOM ARE PALE, dusty green. I can see the pits and bumps of cinder blocks under the paint, the smooth mortar both separating and holding the blocks together. The fluorescent lights in the ceiling are too bright for the room and make a faint, high-pitched buzzing sound. My head no longer aches from what happened yesterday, but I try not to touch the bruise.

This is supposed to be punishment, but actually I'm relieved to be away from everybody at school. It's quiet in here with Mrs. Johnson. The teachers sent down my assignments for today, which weren't all that difficult. I'm already finished with everything but math.

But there's more than just homework. I'm supposed to spend the next five days explaining why I punched Tracy. I know it won't take that long to say Tracy's a jerk, but maybe I can stretch it out. Mrs. Johnson gave me this huge spiral notebook and told me to fill it up with everything that happened. She even gave me two new purple pens to use. I think that's kind of odd, because it's almost as if she's rewarding me for being in trouble. She didn't have to give me anything, and I still would have done what she'd asked.

Writing has always been easy for me. Maybe I should be in trouble more often! I take that back. I really don't want to be in trouble at all. Too bad I can't just be like everyone else. But nobody else is in my situation. Nobody else had a sister like Elaine.

Chapter 1

THERE WERE ONLY A FEW WEEKS LEFT IN THE SCHOOL YEAR, and I could hardly wait for fifth grade to be over. But my alarm didn't go off that morning, and I had trouble tying my hair back, so I was late for breakfast. As I slid into my chair at the table, I accidentally bumped Elaine with my right elbow. She balled her left hand into a fist and punched my shoulder. Then, picking a long strand of my brown, curly hair from her sleeve, she sneered and spat out, "Shedding dogs aren't allowed at the table."

"Then what are you doing there?" Brian asked from where he stood by the sink, eating leftover cold pizza.

Elaine rolled her eyes and picked at her waffle. "You can't expect me to eat this," she complained to Mom, who waited by the toaster for more to spring up.

"Sure I can." Mom snared two hot waffles from the toaster. She put them on a plate, poured syrup on top, and handed the stack over to me.

"Thanks, Mom," I said and picked up my fork. Out of the corner of my eye, I saw Elaine mouthing my words and bobbing her head.

Dad came in. "Sit down," he said to Brian as he took his own seat.

"Don't you sit by me," Elaine said to Brian. "You're disgusting."

Mom and Dad gave her stern looks, but she ignored them and glared at Brian, who sat across from her. While Mom and Dad were talking to each other, he looked right at Elaine and opened his mouth. We could both see the half-eaten cheese and sausage in there. I laughed, but Elaine shouted "Stop it!" and slapped her hand on the table. She tried to kick him, but he scooted his chair back just in time.

"Your nose ring looks beautiful when you're angry," Brian teased.

"Knock it off," Dad warned.

"Some of us just aren't morning people," Brian said lightly.

Elaine dropped her fork, and it clattered on the plate. "Dad," she whined, "why do I have to eat this *garbage* for breakfast?"

Dad sipped his orange juice and smacked his lips before answering. "Because this is *good* garbage—fresh picked from the neighbor's trash just this morning."

"Mmmm, garbage good." I chewed and leaned away from Elaine, but she punched my shoulder again anyway.

"Just eat," Mom said and sat down to her own breakfast.

Elaine crossed her arms. "No."

Mom shrugged and looked across the table at Dad. "You'll get hungry sometime," she said calmly.

"Not here."

"Well, I'm not pulling over at the gas station so you can get some doughnuts and chocolate milk," Brian said and swigged his orange juice.

"You're not taking me to school again in that old thing," Elaine said.

"Yes, he is." Dad stabbed at his waffle. "You forgot to go to school yesterday, so Brian's taking you today." He looked at Brian. "If there's a problem, I want to know about it," he said firmly.

"I was *at school* yesterday." Elaine glared at Dad.

"Could you be more specific?" Mom asked.

"What are you doing—spying on me?"

Mom shrugged. "When necessary."

"You can't expect to skip class and just get away with it," Brian said. He sounded a lot like Dad. "If you do what you're supposed to do, then Mom and Dad leave you alone." He crossed his arms and looked squarely at Elaine.

Mom nodded.

Elaine's face turned red, and she shook her head from side to side. Her shiny, blond hair flew across her face. It was her silent tantrum, the one she had when she knew she was wrong but was still mad anyway.

It was getting late, so I got up to grab my jacket and purple backpack from my bedroom. By the time I got back to the kitchen, Brian and Elaine were gone, and Dad was just leaving. Mom stood over the garbage disposal, scraping Elaine's waffle into it.

I hugged Mom from behind as she flipped the switch. She was tense.

"Aren't you glad she's not a twin?" I asked, hoping that would lighten things up.

Mom laughed raggedly. "Aren't you glad you're not her mother?"

I didn't know what to make of that, so I went

over to my backpack and reshuffled my homework.

"I'm sorry, Gina," Mom said as she loaded the dishwasher. "I'm glad to be Elaine's mother. She just doesn't reward me for it very often."

"She doesn't reward anybody very often." I zipped the backpack shut.

Mom closed the dishwasher and smiled at me. "Can I give you a ride to school, sweetie?"

I shook my head. "No, it's out of your way."

"Not today it isn't," she invited.

"Don't worry, Mom. I'll be all right." I smiled and hugged her again. "It's nice out, and I want to walk."

Mom nodded and brushed her wavy, auburn hair back from her forehead. The nervous gesture gave her away.

"I'll be fine. I promise," I said and headed out the door.

As I hurried to school, I tried to clear Elaine out of my head. As far back as I could remember, she had been mean and just gotten worse as time passed. I thought back to an argument that Elaine once had with our parents. On that morning, Elaine was supposed to walk me to kindergarten. . . .

IT HAD BEEN A PERFECT LATE-SUMMER MORNING. THE leaves stirred softly in the fresh, cool breeze, the air was clear, and the sky was blue. As Elaine and I had walked along the neighborhood sidewalks, the first thing she'd asked me was if I wanted to run away from home with her.

"We could go right now," she said. "No one would even know until school got out. We would be far away by then."

I shook my head no. Every time Elaine and my parents argued, she thought she should run away.

"Fine," she sniffed. "Stay here and rot. Someday I'll be far away and really happy, and you'll be stuck here. And you know what? If you call me on the phone, I'll hang up on you."

I shrugged. "I'll get your room and your stuff." That usually put an end to her complaining.

"There's nothing there I want," she snapped at me and walked faster.

I couldn't keep up with her. She never even turned around to see if I was still behind her. When we came to a corner, she didn't check both ways or look to see that I had crossed safely behind her. At first I struggled to catch up but then wondered if I really wanted to walk with her when she was this grouchy. We were almost at school anyway.

When I got to the playground of Hawthorne School, I stood near the swings, looking at all the different kids playing and talking to each other. Then I remembered Elaine. Where was she? I stood on tiptoe in my stiff, new shoes and glimpsed her walking across the playground to the big kids' side. She didn't even say good-bye to me.

BUT TODAY I DIDN'T FEEL LEFT BEHIND. I WAS CALMER BY the time I got to the playground of Hawthorne School, which was kind of a nice place, but even so, I couldn't wait to go to Lexington Middle School next year.

I found Mary Ann, and we hung around the bicycle racks until the bell rang. Mr. Swayze, our teacher, made us line up like first graders before entering the building.

"This is old," I whispered to her while Mr. Swayze corrected the out-of-liners.

"Yeah, like we're going to be tested on it," she said back.

"A failing grade to those who can't stand in line," I said.

"Gina, we can't go in until you quiet down," called Mr. Swayze from his spot near the door.

"Take your time," whispered Mary Ann.

We finally went in.

AFTER SOCIAL STUDIES AND MATH CAME ENGLISH. WE HAD been writing different kinds of poetry, and today Mr. Swayze wanted us to read one of our poems to the class. Nobody wanted to do it.

He held up his hands. "It's not that bad," he said over our moans. "Every form of literature must have an audience in order to be valid." He pointed to the clock. "You have thirty seconds to make a selection."

He called on Michelle first and asked her to come up to the front of the class. Her shoes made little squeaking sounds as she passed my desk. She glanced around the room, nervously looked down at her folder, and cleared her throat. Her mouth opened, but no sound came out. She shook her head and blinked but couldn't begin. Her eyes glimmered with tears.

The shuffling and giggling coming from the class made things worse. I sat there and wished that she would recite anything at all, even a grocery list.

Mr. Swayze should have excused her, but he didn't. He just looked at her calmly through his thick glasses as if she would recover any minute and carry on.

Finally, she looked at him and mumbled, "I can't do it." She quickly returned to her seat and put her head down. Everyone turned and stared at her.

Mr. Swayze didn't say anything, but he made a little mark with his pen on a piece of paper.

"Gina," he called out, "your turn."

I jumped and looked at him. He waved his pen toward the front of the room.

Well, get it over with, I thought and stepped to

the head of the class. I folded the front of my purple folder to the back and hung onto it with both hands. Suddenly I remembered being a little kid in swim class with my red foam kickboard. It was rounded on one end like a tombstone, and I was supposed to hold it out at arm's length to keep afloat while I learned to kick.

Gripping the folder to keep afloat as I stood there in front of everyone, I looked down at the open page and read:

Brownie

Soft, warm, chewy square
Right out of the oven, with
A cold glass of milk.

It was a perfect poem. Mom had been baking brownies one afternoon, and I was sitting at the kitchen table doing my homework, which was to write a haiku. The rich, chocolaty smell was unbearable. The thought of rinsing down a warm brownie with a tall glass of icy-cold milk drove me crazy. So after they came out of the oven and I had eaten a big square one and gulped that cold milk, I wrote about my experience. Mr. Swayze had told us to write about familiar things, and I knew that brownie very well.

Well, somebody in class thought my poem was funny, because I heard laughter. Then Barbara, who hasn't been my friend since third grade, said, "She probably ate the whole pan."

That made everybody crack up. I felt my face burn. I knew I wasn't as thin as she was, but suddenly I felt like a whale.

I looked over at Mr. Swayze. He marked something on that piece of paper and didn't seem to notice. In the meantime, the whole class was snickering at me.

I couldn't just stand there and be silent. That would be like admitting I was fat, and I wasn't. So I looked squarely at Barbara and, in my most deadly voice, said what Elaine had told me once when she was really mad at me: "I'll beat you."

The words came out meaner than I thought they would. Everybody quieted down, and Mr. Swayze looked up.

"Gina," he said loudly, "go to the hall."

My face grew hotter. I looked angrily at Mr. Swayze and then tossed my folder onto my desk, but it slid off and hit the floor. I didn't mean to toss the folder like that, but now it looked like I was having a temper tantrum. I left the room, wishing I could slam the door behind me.

I sat in the hall for a long time, feeling like an idiot. Barbara should have been kicked out, too. It wasn't fair that she made fun of me and my poem. I looked down at my legs and felt my arms. I wasn't that much bigger than the other girls. And I only ate one brownie that day. Brian had hogged the rest.

The lunch bell rang. Teachers called out their last instructions of the morning. My classroom door burst open, and the kids came out, talking and joking. Some people called out "Brownie!" and laughed at me.

I was petrified. Had they made fun of me in there? Was that why I had sat out here all this time?

A long time ago, when I was a little kid, Brian had teased me by calling me Fruit. I had been wearing a dress and turning somersaults in the front yard. Every time I turned over, he could see my underwear, which were printed with pictures of fruit. It was almost funny, but it made me mad. Mom told me to ignore him.

But he kept calling me Fruit, even when his friends were over. The day *they* started calling me Fruit, I socked Brian. I really meant to hit him right in the mouth, but my aim went wild, and I punched his forehead instead. His friends laughed, but Brian looked surprised. He didn't call me names after that and neither did his friends.

"Aren't you going to talk to Mr. Swayze?" Mary Ann asked as she came out of the room.

I grabbed my jacket. "No."

"But you can't just leave!" she called after me.

Chapter 2

THE AIR WAS FRESH AND COOL, BUT I DIDN'T ENJOY THE walk home. My head was so full of what had happened in class that I left my jacket on even after I felt warm.

I snuck through the neighbors' yards, hoping that no one would see me coming home so early.

When I came around the corner of the garage, Mom's and Dad's cars were in the driveway. Behind them were two police cars.

I ducked back. Could they arrest a kid for leaving school without permission? My legs felt quivery, so I sat down on the damp ground. What were they telling my parents? Would it be better to hide or come out?

As I was thinking it over, the back door opened. Two policemen stepped out of the house, put their caps on their heads, and got in their cars and drove away.

Maybe the school had called them, and Mom and Dad were so alarmed that they both came home from work. I must be in huge trouble. It would be better to explain what had happened before they got any angrier. My legs felt like jelly as I walked to the back door.

Carefully, I pulled the screen door open, then turned the knob on the inside door and let myself in. The kitchen smelled like coffee. That never happened unless company came over.

Four mugs sat by the sink. The coffee maker was still on, and the bitter smell of overdone brew drifted toward me. I turned it off and tiptoed to the living room, where I could hear Mom and Dad talking.

The curtains were open, letting in mild, clear sunlight. Even here the scent of coffee was still strong, but the air smelled like aftershave and ink as well. As I stood in the entryway, I saw the back of the sofa, where they sat close together.

Mom's hair was messed up. Her shoulders buckled, and she sobbed into her hands. I had never heard her cry before.

Dad sat to her right and looked out the window. He was taking deep breaths, which was his way of keeping calm. He put an arm around Mom's shoulders, then glanced back at me standing there. Nodding in my direction, he squeezed Mom gently and whispered, "Gina."

She wiped her hands on her slacks and stood up to face me. Her makeup had been cried away. Her eyes were dark underneath, and her nose had turned a raw red. I noticed new wrinkles in her forehead. Her mouth and jaw were set, as if she was trying hard to be tough. But her eyes gave her away—they were starry crystal blue edged with pain.

Mom and Dad could not be this upset at me for leaving school. I asked, "What is it?"

Mom took a deep breath. She looked at me and opened her mouth, but nothing came out. She closed her mouth and hugged herself.

Dad stood up and put his arm around Mom's shoulders again. "Elaine skipped school and was in a car accident with another student this morning," he said. Tears trickled down his face, and his voice carried the dull, gray burden of grief. "She didn't survive."

His words were so heavy that I could almost see them tumbling out of his mouth and rolling toward me like tired old cannonballs.

The breath left my lungs, and I gasped—the air

had grown brittle with shock. My jacket suffocated me. I didn't know what to say, but inside something felt so terrible and strong that I began to cry. I walked over to Mom and hugged her around the waist.

Brian came home from school a little while after that. Dad sat us around the kitchen table and told us what had happened. Elaine had gone to school with Brian but then left with a boy. They were driving out in the country when the car went too fast around a curve and hit a tree. The other student had died, too.

"Dave Kipsey," Brian said. Mom had left the kitchen after making more coffee. She came back carrying a box of tissues, placed them on the table, and shuffled away.

Dad looked at Brian and tilted his head to one side. "Did you know him?"

Brian poured himself a cup of coffee and held out the pot to Dad, who shook his head. He sat down and swirled his mug around before answering. "Not really. We called him Skippy because he skipped classes so much."

Dad glanced at me before asking Brian, "Do you know much about him?"

Brian shook his head and looked at his coffee. Tears rolled down his cheeks. "I wish that I had followed her, made sure she went to class. . . ." His voice cracked.

He reached for a tissue and wiped it across his eyes.

Dad nodded and touched Brian's arm. "It's not your fault. It was an accident," he said gently.

I reached for a new tissue. The box was like a deck of cards among us, and we took turns drawing from it. As I listened to them talk, I felt grief hollow out my insides. Tears flooded down my face then mysteriously dried up. But they always came back. I couldn't stop it from happening.

Mom had given me a cup of coffee with a lot of milk and sugar, which tasted good, but it wasn't what I wanted. I finished it and filled my cup with water. I was so thirsty.

Dad sat to my left. I didn't want to stare, but he looked so different that I couldn't help it. His eyes were puffy underneath, and he had that same set to his mouth that Mom had. His brown hair was rumpled from running his fingers through it. It must be a family thing, I thought. He couldn't look either of us in the eye for very long.

Brian didn't say anything. He looked at his coffee an awful lot. Maybe he wanted to say something to Dad in private.

I looked over at Elaine's empty chair and rubbed my shoulder where she had punched me that morning. I tried to picture her sitting there again, but nothing happened. I didn't even see a ghost.

I left my mug by the sink and went to look for Mom. She was just hanging up the telephone in their bedroom. As I sat on the bed, she looked curiously at me. "Why did you leave school?"

"Huh?"

"I just called to say we had a family emergency, and the secretary told me that you weren't in class this afternoon. Why did you come home early?"

I had forgotten all about Barbara and her stupid comment. Suddenly it wasn't important. I wasn't about to bother her with the whole story at a time like this. I figured I could handle it myself.

I shrugged. "I was mad at Barbara because she said something, and Mr. Swayze didn't hear her, but he heard what I said back to her."

Mom nodded but didn't answer. The telephone rang, and we jumped. She answered it and spoke briefly. "Yes," she said flatly. She listened for a moment, then said, "I'm really not ready to talk about it yet. But thank you for calling." She hung up.

"Who was that?" I asked.

Mom sighed. "A friend of hers."

We always got calls from Elaine's friends. Without thinking, I said the dumbest thing ever. "Why didn't you take a message?"

It was as if I had stabbed her in the heart. She groaned, and new tears fell down her cheeks. They made hollow plopping noises on the bedspread, like sad rain.

I just sat there, feeling stupid. I didn't want to risk saying anything more, but when Mom came around the bed, I stood up and hugged her. I was thankful that she hugged me back.

Chapter 3

MOM AND DAD WENT OUT THE NEXT DAY TO MAKE arrangements while Brian stayed home with me. We were both supposed to go through our closets while they were gone and find two sets of clothes we could wear to the visitation and funeral.

I got out a purple dress with long sleeves. It might be a little warm, but it would have to do. I found my good black shoes and put them on the bed. I couldn't find anything else that was appropriate. Mom wouldn't want to go to the mall right now. Elaine had so many clothes that I didn't think anyone would notice if I borrowed something of hers.

Her door was shut. I slowly turned the knob and walked in, remembering all the times she'd yelled "Get out of here!" at me. Her bed was unmade, as usual, and I could see the rumpled dents where she'd slept. Her pillow was punched flat between the bed and the wall. I looked around and felt a little embarrassed at seeing the mess. But she had no way of knowing she wouldn't come back. I clapped my hands to break the mood.

I went to her closet and opened it. We had different tastes in clothing. I liked mine loose and colorful, and she liked dark clothes that fit her closely. She and Mom had gotten into some royal arguments about what Elaine wore to school. Mom always won, but it tired her out, and Elaine always smiled afterward, as though she had enjoyed the fight.

I scooted some things aside and came across a dark green dress Elaine had bought before going on a date one time. It was short sleeved and had a high neck. The fabric was velvety and heavy, with little dark green flowers.

Carrying the dress, I went back to my room and shut the door. I traded my T-shirt and jeans for the dress and looked into my mirror. I pulled the fabric out at my sides, seeing that there really wasn't that much extra. Turning around, I looked at the back view. It looked like a big, pretty shirt that went down to my knees. I could wear my black tights with it. I took it off and laid it on the bed.

When Mom came home and saw it, she clamped her mouth shut. Finally she asked, "Are you sure you want to wear this?"

"If you say it's all right. The only other thing I could find was my purple dress."

Mom nodded and sighed. "I guess so."

I hugged her carefully. "I'll put it back afterward."

She put one hand on top of my head and rested it there. Then she turned and left my room without comment.

DURING THE NEXT AFTERNOON, PEOPLE ARRIVED WITH casseroles, trays of cold cuts and cheese, and cakes. I couldn't believe all the food that showed up, but it didn't last long. At first I loaded up on the desserts. Then I got caked out and made sandwiches.

Finally we drove to the funeral home for the visitation. Elaine's casket was closed, and it really bothered me not to see her. There was a large school picture of her (taken before she got the nose ring) in a pretty gold frame on top of the polished wooden casket. Pink rosebuds were scattered around it, and there were large vases of flowers everywhere. Most of the flower arrangements had little cards placed in them. I was surprised to see one from Mr. Swayze.

A lot of people came to pay their respects. It was weird, like a sad party. Mom and Dad stood near the casket and talked to people, and Brian and I stood a few steps away from them. Elaine's friends came, but they stood together like flocks of birds at the back of the room. Grandma had come, along with my aunts and uncles. There were cousins everywhere, but they didn't visit often and were nearly strangers to me. So I sat by Grandma and held her hand for a while.

I was surprised by all the talking that went on. People made comments to each other and to us. I really didn't know what to say, and so I said "Thank you" when people told me that they were sorry about Elaine.

I went over to Brian when there were too many adults in the room. He took care of me and included me in conversations with his friends when they came by. He hugged me when I cried and got me a piece of cake and a cup of coffee with sugar and milk. He also looked after Grandma. Nobody came from my school, but that was all right. I didn't want to see them.

The funeral was the next day. A man said some nice things about Elaine—and I let myself believe them, but I could tell that he didn't know what she was really like—and then he said a prayer. We walked past the casket one more time. I touched its smooth surface, wishing I could hold her hand instead, even if she would shake it away angrily. Thinking about that made me cry. Brian put an arm around my shoulder and led me away.

It was a pretty day. The sun was bright, and the air smelled like freshly cut grass and blooming flowers. The green dress was just a little warm, but I hugged myself and grabbed at the soft, loose fabric, carefully pulling it away from my warm body.

We had all followed the hearse to the cemetery and waited while Dad, Brian, and some uncles carried the casket to the grave site. They placed it on a stand. Another man had brought the pink rosebuds and arranged them again on the lid. Everyone stood on the fake green grass around the casket and held hands while the man who had spoken about Elaine said another prayer.

There was a lot of hugging then, and we leaned on each other as we returned to our cars. I looked back at Elaine's coffin, gleaming in the sun. It was hard to think of her inside it. I especially didn't want to think about her going into the ground.

At home there was more company and more food. Brian brought me a plate with a thick roast beef sandwich, chips, and a piece of cake. Gradually everybody finished up and said their good-byes. The house quieted down.

Brian and I cleaned up the kitchen while Mom and Dad sat in the living room. I asked Brian why the casket was closed.

He made me sit at the table. "The accident was really bad," he said in a low voice. "She was thrown out through the windshield when the car hit the tree."

I didn't want to imagine that. I looked down at my hands and changed the subject a little. "Was she wearing a seat belt?"

He shook his head. "I don't know. Probably not."

I nodded. "Were they drinking?" I had seen a lot of commercials begging people not to drink and drive.

"Yes." Brian looked at me squarely then looked down at his hands.

A cold, gray weight settled in my chest. "That was stupid," I said. "How could she be so stupid?"

"How could they *both* be so stupid?" He reached for a tissue and handed it over to me. Acting like an idiot had cost Elaine her life. It was senseless. I sobbed jaggedly into my hands. Brian knelt by my chair and held me close.

Chapter 4

THE SILENCE THAT FOLLOWED ELAINE'S DEATH WAS TERRIBLE. I would have given anything to argue with her or hear music thumping from her bedroom. There was nothing but the air that she'd moved through.

Everybody in the house was broken. We still spoke to each other, but sadness hung over everything. Brian didn't show me the food going around in his mouth anymore, and I didn't kick him under the table. Mom and Dad made small talk at dinner but didn't really pay attention to what was said.

I began to understand what grief is: it's missing someone who's never coming back. I looked at

Elaine's black comb in the bathroom and plucked a strand of blond hair from it. I held it up and thought about keeping it in my jewelry box. But how was I supposed to remember all of her by just looking at a piece of hair? I carefully lowered it into the trash.

Right after I woke up one morning, I pretended to be dead. I lay under the sheets, folded my hands across my stomach, and closed my eyes. I let my breath run out. Mom and Dad were talking softly in their bedroom. A few cars drove down the street. Birds sang, and dogs barked. Then I had to breathe. I lay there for a little while and listened to the sounds of life all around me. What was it like for Elaine? Did she miss us? Where did she go? Was it dark? I stayed in bed until Dad knocked on my door to get me up.

On the first Saturday without Elaine, Mom and Dad announced that the front and back yards needed work. They said it would be good for us to get outside. After breakfast they drove to the nursery to buy flowers and vegetables, and Brian headed off to the garage to mess with the lawn mower. I faked a stomachache and sat inside as the house emptied out. I took Elaine's old school picture—the one Mom and Dad had taken to the funeral home—off the shelf in the living room and sat down on the sofa with it. She looked happy and pretty in the gold frame. Her hair was tucked behind her ears, and her brown eyes sparkled. She smiled, and her whole face was bright. She wore a turquoise blue sweater and long silver earrings with little bells on them. I sat there and memorized her face.

Suddenly I wondered where that sweater and those earrings were. I put the picture back on the shelf and peeked out the kitchen window to make sure Brian was still in the garage. Nobody was looking, so I snuck down the hall to Elaine's room. It had been only a few days since we had buried her, but the air in her bedroom was already stale. The window shade was pulled up, and pale yellow sunlight came in through the flowered curtains. The bed was still unmade.

The walls had been painted a light blue, but they were faded and marred with holes. Elaine had started to hang up some posters, but Mom and Dad didn't like her doing it without permission. So she went out to the used music store in town and bought old albums with disgusting pictures on them. She hung those up instead.

"YOU SAID NOT TO HANG UP POSTERS," ELAINE HAD SAID and smirked when Mom saw them.

"That's not what I said," Mom told her. "I said not to hang up posters without permission."

"You didn't say anything about album covers."

An intense argument had followed. It ended when Elaine smiled and said, "Just stay out of my room if you don't like it." I was amazed to hear Mom agree to that.

At first I thought Mom had caved in. But that wasn't the case. The following Saturday she left the vacuum cleaner right outside Elaine's door. It stayed there most of the day until Elaine grumbled and hustled it back to the linen closet. Mom just rolled it in front of her door again. Then Elaine plugged it in and left it running in her room, but Mom was wise to that, too. I was peeking around Mom when she opened the door and found the vacuum cleaner just sitting in the middle of the room, humming away. Elaine sat on her bed, painting her toenails and listening to her headphones.

Mom turned off the vacuum. Elaine clicked off her headphones and said coolly, "I thought you were going to stay out of here."

"I thought you wouldn't give me a reason to come in," Mom shot back. "If you want to play games, I can play them, too, and I'll win. If you want me to come in here and vacuum your floor, Elaine, that stuff comes off the walls. It's as simple as that."

She paused to look around at the piles of clothes, the unmade bed, and the crumpled papers lying by the overflowing wastebasket. "Come to think of it, honey, why don't you start taking them down now? Obviously you need me to straighten up in here."

Elaine's eyes narrowed to slits. "It's *my* room."

"In *my* house. Straighten up this mess, and you can keep your album covers. I'll respect your privacy when you respect my rules for being neat and clean." Mom calmly shut the door behind her, and I heard Elaine angrily click the headphones back on.

THAT HAD HAPPENED A FEW MONTHS AGO. NOW I LOOKED around the room, hearing only the sound of my own breathing. I felt like a burglar, but I had to know about the sweater and earrings.

I opened a dresser drawer and found the sweater neatly folded. I touched its soft fabric, carefully smoothing it out before I gently closed the drawer.

I looked in Elaine's jewelry box for the earrings. They weren't there, but I did find some earrings I had given her when I was younger. They were little yellow buttons with smiley faces on them. Elaine had laughed and never told me if she liked them or not. I was always afraid she'd stick one in her nose after she'd gotten it pierced.

Suddenly I wanted those earrings for myself. I carried them into my own room to put in my jewelry box, which is also where I kept my money.

THE RULE WAS THAT MOM AND DAD PAID TWENTY DOLLARS if any of us got straight As. I had tried my best earlier that year, even doing an extra-credit report on gerbils, and I finally earned those As.

When Dad came home from work that night, I ran right up to him. "Look! I did it!" I waved my report card at him as he hung up his coat in the front closet.

"Let me see. Oh, straight As!" He looked over every subject and grade, reading it all aloud and making a big deal of it. I stood proudly on tiptoe. Then he handed the report card back and gave me a giant hug. "I owe you some money," he said grandly. He reached for his wallet and took out the freshest, crispest twenty-dollar bill I had ever seen.

I took it by the edges, being careful not to wrinkle it. I inhaled the inky, luxurious scent of money. My eyes crossed as I looked at Andrew Jackson's portrait up close. Off to the side, I saw a little ghost image of him. Carefully I rubbed the bill between my fingers, exploring the crisp, heavy quality of the paper. It had crazy little red and blue threads woven into it.

"It has veins," I said, awestruck. Of course I had held money before, but this was the first time I'd held my own twenty. I looked up at Dad. "Thank you."

He smiled down at me. "I'm very proud of you," he said warmly.

I hugged him around the middle and ran to my room to put the new bill in my jewelry box. Because I didn't own much jewelry, I kept other valuable stuff in there. It was a marvelous dark green with a border of gold leaves—more like a treasure chest than a jewelry box. When I opened it, a hinged tray attached to the lid came up. A little music would play, which was silly, but it made a good burglar alarm, so I always left it wound up. It was lined with shiny, dark green velvet. There were larger compartments in the bottom and smaller compartments in the hinged tray. Most were empty.

I kept the jewelry box on my dresser on a lacy handkerchief that Grandma had given me before she moved away. When I picked up the box, everything inside shifted and rattled. It gave me a feeling of wealth and history. I took the box over to my bed and unlocked it with the little brass key I kept hidden in one of my books.

The familiar, velvety smell drifted up as I opened the box. I examined each item. My Mickey Mouse ring had lost its gold metal finish, but I wasn't about to throw that away. Occasionally I still wore the watch that I had been given on my eighth birthday. I lined up all the pretty stones on the bedspread. I also had a few half-dollars and ten silver-dollar coins. Mom and Dad didn't give us a regular allowance, but if a long time passed and I didn't ask for anything, Dad sometimes gave me another silver dollar for my jewelry box.

I put the twenty in one of the bottom compartments and stacked the dollar coins on top of it. The half-dollars had their own parking space, and in they went. The stones went in next to them. Mickey Mouse went back in the top tray.

Someone was watching. I turned and saw Elaine standing in the doorway, her head tilted to one side. She smiled and came into my room, sat on my bed, and picked up my watch.

"I need to put that back," I said to her. I held out my hand.

"Piece of junk." She shrugged and tossed my watch back on the bedspread. I made myself pick it up slowly, not showing how nervous I was. I closed the lid and held the key tightly in my hand. I didn't want her to see my hiding place for it. I turned my back, put the box back on the dresser, and slipped the key under it.

"You keep some neat stuff in that box," Elaine said slyly, tracing the sun and moon patterns on my bedspread.

I was uncomfortable. "It's just stuff," I said.

She looked up from the bedspread and pointed a polished black fingernail at me. "Don't lie to me," she said coldly. Her brown eyes were dull and flat. Her mouth puckered angrily. "I know what you have in there."

I struggled to keep my voice calm. "If you don't want to be nice, you can just leave."

"I'm planning on it," she said icily and walked across the hall to her room. The door slammed shut.

NOW THAT DAY CAME BACK CLEARLY IN MY MIND AS I LIFTED my jewelry box from my dresser and missed the sound of my dollar and half-dollar coins rattling around.

I brought the box over to my bed and unlocked it. All my money was gone! My heart raced as I put the earrings in the top tray, locked the box, and put the key in a new hiding place. I marched right back over to Elaine's room.

There is nothing worse than being angry at a dead person. There is nowhere for the anger to go. I wanted to mess up her bed or her clothes or something, but she wasn't around to see me do it. I opened the closet doors and saw a white plastic bag with "Elaine

Beck" printed neatly on it. I pulled it down from the shelf and got into it.

Her brown purse was in there. I shook it and heard a metallic clinking sound. I searched all the little zippered pockets until I found the source of the noise: my dollar coins—some of them, anyway. I took them out and laid them on the floor. Then I pulled out her wallet. It had fifteen dollars in it. I couldn't prove that she'd stolen the twenty-dollar bill Dad had given me for getting good grades, but it certainly looked as though she had. I set the bills by the coins. Then I rooted through the rest of her wallet, finding pictures of her friends and a lot of telephone numbers. There were a few ticket stubs from movies. Way in the back, I found something that made my heart stop cold.

It was my school picture from kindergarten. I looked at myself as a smug five-year-old, smiling crookedly for the camera. My hair was in pigtails tied with purple ribbons. I turned the picture over. She had written "My sister Gina" on the back in green ink. If she had hated me so much, why had she carried a picture of me?

How did her purse get into the closet? I peered into the plastic bag and saw her brown hiking boots and a pair of thick socks. I sat back on my heels. Of course they would have sent her things home from the hospital. I turned the bag around and saw the design for St. John Hospital. This must have been all they would give Mom and Dad. I had been blind to everything but getting revenge.

I looked at the money on the floor. It had to be mine, but it didn't mean anything now. I crammed it all back into her purse and put the bag back on the shelf. I walked into my bedroom, closed the door behind me, and flopped down on the bed. I felt like crying, but my stomach hurt too much.

Chapter 5

WE WENT BACK TO SCHOOL EXACTLY ONE WEEK AFTER Elaine was buried. Mary Ann was the only one who said anything. She was sitting on her bike when I walked by the rack.

"Hey," she said and began wrestling with her padlock.

"Hey," I said and waited for her to lock up her bike.

"I thought you'd ride today."

I shook my head. Riding would have given me less time to think before getting to school.

"Sorry about Elaine." She kept her eyes on the padlock and chain.

"Thank you," I said automatically. I looked around at the other students running and playing. It looked just like any other morning on the playground, but somehow it felt different. Everything seemed to have changed after Elaine died.

In class, Mr. Swayze said he was glad to see me back, but nobody else said anything about it. That was all right, because I didn't really feel like talking.

Mrs. Thomas, the counselor, saw me a few days later. She came during P.E. class. We were playing softball, which wasn't my favorite sport. I had trouble figuring out how to hit the ball. The people in the outfield chanted "Shoo, shoo, shoo" every time I swung the bat, and that was annoying.

"We're glad you're back, Gina," Mrs. Thomas said warmly as we walked into the school and down the hall to her office.

I shrugged. Tell that to the people on my side in the softball game.

"It certainly is a lovely afternoon," she continued.

I nodded my head. "Yeah."

"School will be out soon. Do you have any plans for the summer?"

"No, not really," I answered. Actually, I planned to ride my bike to the library and use the Internet. I liked the Web sites that had games. There were magazines I liked, too, and plenty of books to read.

Mrs. Thomas led me into her cozy, colorful office. She had two beanbag chairs, one orange and one yellow, and three wooden chairs painted blue, red, and green. The chairs and beanbags were set so that they faced each other in a circle. Holding them together was a round, colorful rag rug. The floor spreading out beneath the rug was painted a medium blue. The chairs and rug looked like a giant lily pad floating in a pond.

Mrs. Thomas sat in one of the wooden chairs. "Have a seat, Gina," she said and waved at the other chairs.

I thought about the orange beanbag but decided on a chair instead. I didn't want to look like a goof sliding around on the floor in front of the counselor.

"I'm really sorry about your sister," she said. "What was her name?" She leaned forward and looked closely at me.

I tilted my head to the side. "Elaine," I said softly.

"Can you tell me about it?" She dipped her head, encouraging me to speak.

"It was sad." I didn't want to say much more. I didn't know Mrs. Thomas very well.

She nodded her head again, as if I had said something valuable. "Do you miss her?"

I nodded, not trusting myself to speak. My throat tightened. I looked out the window at the cars in the teachers' parking lot.

"It's O.K." She leaned closer and waited for me to say something more.

I remembered a few years ago when a stray cat had come into the backyard. It was skinny and black and fearful. I was sitting in the wading pool, eating a bologna sandwich and watching the cat as it slunk through the shadows under the bushes. I peeled off a bite of bologna and tossed it over there. The cat crouched with suspicion. After a moment it crept toward the soiled bologna and gulped it down. I tossed over another piece, but the cat continued on its way through the shadows and out of our yard.

Mrs. Thomas was tossing bologna at me. If I started to talk about Elaine, I wouldn't be able to finish until the end. There was too much to tell, and the telling would make me cry. I nodded my head and continued looking out the window. If I looked down, tears might gather, and then they'd fall, and Mrs. Thomas would have what she wanted. She would probably tell Mr. Swayze all about it.

"Can you tell me more?"

"Not right now." I struggled to keep my voice even.

Mrs. Thomas waited quietly. The round yellow clock on the wall ticked. Finally she said, "Well, if you ever need me, just let Mr. Swayze know, and I'll be happy to see you." She slowly rose from her chair. I started to feel guilty about not cooperating with her, but then I remembered that black cat.

Luckily she didn't walk me back to P.E. I ducked into the girls' bathroom and locked myself in a stall. I leaned against the door and lost count of my deep breaths.

SCHOOLWORK TURNED OUT TO BE A RELIEF. THERE WAS SO much to make up at first that I didn't have much time to think about anything else. And soon it became a challenge to figure out how Mr. Swayze wanted the assignments done. The good grades were rewarding.

Elaine was still on my mind though. Sometimes a memory popped into my head—sort of like a TV commercial. These interruptions broke my concentration and bothered me sometimes, but they took my mind off the fact that Elaine was gone.

One day Mr. Swayze was yelling at us because everyone did poorly on a social studies test. I suddenly had a commercial of the time I pestered Elaine by eavesdropping while she was talking with some guy on the phone. I had picked up the phone in Mom and Dad's room and made gross kissing noises into it. When I said "Love me! Squeeze me!" Elaine threw down her phone and chased me through the house.

I made it as far as the kitchen before I slipped on the linoleum and skidded into the refrigerator. Then she was on me, kicking and screaming swearwords. Mom had to break it up. My arms were bruised from Elaine's kicks and my back was, too, from colliding with the refrigerator, but it had been awfully fun to make her mad.

So there I was, smiling away while Mr. Swayze was yelling, and he suddenly stared at me and said, "What's so funny, Gina? Did I say something funny?"

I blinked at him.

He glared at me.

"What's so funny about flunking a test?" he yelled. The air was white with his anger.

I scooted down in my seat and said, "I didn't flunk it." That was true. I'd gotten a D.

"Get out!" he yelled.

My legs shook as I left the room. My stomach was in knots. Curious teachers peered from nearby classrooms. When they saw me in the hall, they shook their heads and turned their backs. At that moment, I didn't like them anymore. It was none of their business.

Mr. Swayze followed me out. "What's your problem?" he said sharply. The veins no longer bulged on his forehead, but his face was still really dark. His eyes bugged out behind his glasses.

My voice rushed up from deep inside. "I don't have a problem," I said, crossing my arms. "I didn't flunk the test."

His mouth flattened into an angry line. "That's not what I'm talking about," he said. "If you think you can be disrespectful in my class, you think again."

He hadn't asked me a question, so I didn't say anything to him.

"I can make you miserable for the rest of the year," he bragged. He stood really close to my face, but I wasn't intimidated.

Suddenly my words bubbled up like lava. "I don't think there's anything you can do to make me more miserable." Tears wanted to well up in my eyes, but I didn't want to cry in front of him.

Mr. Swayze straightened up and stepped back. He paused, then said quietly, "I should have known. I'm very sorry, Gina."

I looked at the floor through the tears that had come anyway. A few plopped onto my shoes.

Mr. Swayze put his hand on my shoulder. "Why don't you go to the girls' room for a few minutes?"

he said kindly. “Come back to class, and we’ll go over the test.”

I nodded and walked quickly to the rest room. When I returned to class, the other kids gawked at me. Had they been talking about me? Nobody really knew how I felt. Lucky for them. Quietly I slid into my seat and wished for the year to be over.

Chapter 6

MOM AND DAD THOUGHT I SHOULD STAY HOME MORE THAT summer. Brian had a job as a cashier at the SuperFood, so I was left alone every afternoon. At first I read or watched the trashy talk shows on TV, but then I got bored hanging around the house, and Mom finally gave me a house key.

"If you go anywhere, even just for a bike ride, I want you to call me and let me know where you're going. When you come back, I want you to call me again," she said, shaking the key at me.

"O.K., O.K.," I said impatiently and grabbed the key.

She watched me put the key on my chain. The only other keys I had were for my bike and my jewelry box.

"And if you say you'll be in one place, I'd better not find out you were really somewhere else," she continued.

That hadn't occurred to me, but I didn't let her know that. "Yes, Mother, dear," I said and hugged her.

"If you do anything at all that annoys me, the key and the bike are mine." She pointed her finger at me as she spoke.

Can I breathe now? I thought, but said, "Don't worry, Mom."

She looked at me long and hard, then finally nodded. "And don't roll your eyes at me."

"I didn't!"

"Inside you were," she said and smiled a little.

I rolled my eyes for real. "Glad to get it out," I said.

THE NEXT AFTERNOON, I TRIED TO CALL MARY ANN TO ASK if she could come to the library with me, but nobody answered. I called Mom, then gathered up the books that needed to be returned and stuffed them into my backpack. It was cloudy and a little cool, so I shrugged into my jacket and headed out the door.

It didn't take long to get to the library. I returned the books and checked out some more. As I left I thought what a shame it would be to use all that freedom to go only there and back. A new gift shop had opened right next door. It wouldn't hurt to look around for just a few minutes, so I walked in.

It was wonderful. It smelled good—like vanilla, new carpet, and fresh paint. Soft piano music played while I looked around. The more expensive gifts were in glass cases in the front, but the children's section was in the back, and that's where the stuffed animals were.

I fell in love with a little plush dragon. He was bright green and fuzzy with purple spikes down his back and tail and a bright red tummy. His eyes were small, shiny, and black, and a small orange tongue hung out of his mouth. He fit perfectly into the palm of my hand, where he seemed quite comfortable.

But the price was a lot more than I could afford, thanks to Elaine. I didn't think that the saleswoman would set it aside for me while I begged Mom and Dad for money. But the thought of leaving the dragon was unbearable—there were no others in the store like him.

I looked slyly at the saleswoman, who had rung up a crystal vase and was now wrapping it in white tissue paper as she chatted with the man who had bought it. There was no one else in the shop.

I quickly stuffed the dragon into my jacket pocket.

I knew that it was wrong to steal. But the dragon was so cute, and since Elaine had stolen my money, how could I pay for it?

Could anyone tell I had him? Was his tail hanging out? I moved behind a rack of birthday cards and checked. He made a little round bulge in my pocket, but that was all.

But what if I got caught? I would say I was looking at all the toys and just put this one in my pocket and forgot about it. It was a lame excuse, but I thought it might work.

I walked coolly around the card rack. My knees shook with excitement and nervousness. The vase was now in a pretty emerald green box. The saleswoman and the man were still yakking it up and didn't notice as I slipped out the door. My hands shook as I unlocked my bike. I felt uneasy but didn't dare look around to see if anyone was looking because that would make *me* look suspicious.

I raced home, my backpack spanking my back as I pedaled. I struggled with the kickstand, then let my bike fall to the sidewalk as I ran up the back steps. The back door key wouldn't go in, but then I realized I was holding it upside down.

I ran to my room and shut the door behind me. Where could I keep him? I opened my closet door and looked around, but the closet didn't seem to be the place for him. My bookshelf was filled with paperbacks. I pulled a handful forward, leaving an empty space behind them.

I took the dragon out and petted him for a minute. He had a different attitude now that he'd been kidnapped by me. His colors weren't as bright. He looked disappointed with me, but I refused to believe him. I lowered him into the dark behind the books and sat back on my heels to survey the result. It was too noticeable. I pulled all the books forward. There!

THAT EVENING EVERYTHING WENT DOWNHILL. MOM YELLED at me because I had forgotten to call her when I came home. Then she grounded me from my bike and the key for three days. I moped around after dinner and finally decided to go to bed.

After turning out the lamp on the bookshelf, all I did was think about not paying for the dragon. Well, I thought, Elaine had stolen my money . . . so I had stolen the dragon . . . and that made me no better than Elaine. Instead of having something that I could show off and be happy with, I was hiding a dark secret. I put my head under my pillow and began to worry. If the dragon was discovered, I would have no excuse. How would Mom and Dad punish me?

The only way to make it right was to return him the next day, Saturday. Maybe Mom would need to go to town for something, and I could catch a ride with her.

It was dark and pouring down rain when I woke up in the morning, but I couldn't wait to unshoplift the dragon. I said that there was a book at the library that I had forgotten to check out. Brian offered to drive me.

The dragon felt like a stone in my pocket as we headed toward town. Brian said I could play the car stereo, but I shook my head and said he could choose a station.

"All right, but don't complain." He pushed the button for his favorite music station and turned the volume way, way up. Then he turned his head and gave me his skeleton grin, which showed his bottom teeth. He crossed his sparkly blue eyes and flared his nostrils. I laughed even though I felt nervous and rotten on the inside.

He pulled up by the library. The rain gushed down. I climbed out, casually cradling the dragon pocket. Brian turned down the radio.

"I'll just pull around and find a space," he said.

"O.K." I hoped he wouldn't notice when I ran into the shop instead of the library.

I dashed into the store and looked out the window. Brian was waiting for a parking space.

"May I help you?"

I turned, startled, and looked up into the face of the lady who had been there yesterday. We were alone in the store.

I smiled shyly and said, "No, I'm just looking. It's pretty rainy out."

She nodded. "Good weather for staying indoors. Well, let me know if there's anything I can help you with." She went to the front counter and took out a dustcloth and began polishing the cups and saucers in a glass case.

I casually worked my way to the stuffed animals and turned to the side so that the lady wouldn't see me take the dragon out. When I turned to check on her, she happened to look up at me. Just then the front door opened, jingling the little brass bell. She turned toward the sound, and I quickly took the dragon out of my pocket and stuffed him back on the shelf. He was a little damp but would dry off. I looked sadly at the dragon, wishing he was mine, and then turned.

Brian was right behind me. His arms were crossed, and he towered over me. A few raindrops dripped from his curly red hair onto the floor. His jean jacket was soaked.

"What are you doing?" His voice was soft, dark, and deadly.

I looked at the lady, who had gone back to polishing the merchandise. She didn't seem to hear us.

"Just looking at something," I said quietly.

His eyes drilled into mine. I dared not look away because if I did, he would know I was lying. He stepped back, but his arms were still crossed. "What were you looking at?"

I turned to the toys. "This," I said and pointed to the dragon. I was afraid to touch him now.

"That?" He seemed surprised. He bent and plucked it from the shelf. His hands were big, and the soft little dragon looked very small in his grip. "This is for a kid."

"Yeah, I guess." Suddenly I felt stupid for stealing and trying to blame it on Elaine. I put my hands in my pockets.

He posed the dragon in his hand. "It's a little wet."

"I was holding it." That wasn't exactly a lie.

He pursed his lips and returned the dragon to the shelf. Brian looked at me in silence. Finally he spoke. "So this is why you had to come to the library today."

I looked him square in the eye. "Yes."

"Are you done?"

"Yes."

He walked calmly to the front of the shop, and I followed him. Would he tell on me?

"Thank you," he said to the lady.

"Come again," she called after us.

Brian shot me a look and held the door for me. I started to run through the rain, but he caught my sleeve. "You're getting wet," he said. We walked to his car. I waited while he took his sweet time unlocking my door. Without a word, he started the car and turned off the radio. We didn't speak all the way home.

As we pulled into the driveway, I said, "Thanks for taking me."

He turned the engine off and jingled the keys in his hand.

"Are you going to tell?" I asked nervously.

He measured me with his eyes. "No," he finally said. "But I'll back you up if you want to tell on yourself."

No way was I turning myself in! I looked down at my hands and twisted my fingers together.

"If you do bad things, bad things will happen to you. Don't put Mom and Dad through any more grief." He climbed out into the downpour.

He was right. I hadn't thought about how Mom and Dad might feel if they caught me stealing. I didn't get out of the car right away. After a few minutes, I ran through the rain to the back door.

It was locked. I had to ring the bell and wait for Dad to let me in.

Chapter 7

MARY ANN AND I RODE OUR BIKES A LOT THE REST OF THE summer and talked about starting sixth grade in the fall.

"I hope there are more boys," she said one day as we sat on the swings at Hawthorne School. "And I hope they're better looking."

"I hope it's more interesting," I said.

"Boys are interesting."

"Brian isn't interesting." I swung back and forth just a little.

"Yes he is," she said and suddenly blushed.

"That's disgusting," I said, wrinkling my nose.

"Not to me it isn't." She began to swing, too.

"Well, he's not the only guy out there." The idea of Mary Ann—or anybody else for that matter—being interested in Brian was just too weird.

She shrugged, and we listened to the creaking of the chains as we swung. I looked over at Hawthorne and thought it was a good thing I wouldn't be back there in the fall. After everything with Elaine, it seemed better to start fresh at a new school.

Our class had toured Lexington Middle School at the end of fifth grade. It had two floors, and lockers lined the hallways. Lexington took in students from three other elementary schools. I looked forward to being with more people my age and doing more exciting things.

Mom and I went shopping toward the end of the summer. She wouldn't buy me some of the clothes I wanted. When I fussed about it at the mall, she said, "This is what you're getting. Be glad you're not going to school in your underwear."

"You probably wouldn't get me the underwear I'd want," I grumbled.

Mom smiled. "As long as it came up to your armpits, I'd be happy."

"Yeah, right. Send me to school with a super-wedgy, why don't you?"

"I'll give it to you myself." She snickered.

I quickly learned the fine art of negotiation. I'd pick out something I would never even wear, like a shirt that was cut a little low, and she'd choose something that came up to my chin. From there, we compromised toward something in the middle. I got some things that I wanted with some of her choices thrown in.

"You should wear something pretty in your hair," Mom said as we climbed back into the car to go home.

"Huh?" It sounded like she had been reading one of those teen magazines in the library.

"Well," she said, tilting her head and squinting her eyes, "you could put your hair up instead of letting it run wild." She reached over and gently bunched my hair into a sweeping tail on top of my head. I noticed the worry lines around her eyes and mouth. "How do you keep the knots out?"

"Two words, Mom: de tangler."

She laughed. "That's one word, goofy."

"Can I get my ears pierced?"

"No," she said and let my hair fall down.

I took Mom's advice and practiced twisting my hair around and catching it in a giant purple hair clip. I had grown taller over the summer, and the new hairstyle made me look elegant and mature.

Pierced ears would have been nice. Mom probably said no because Elaine had them, and look what happened to her. The last thing I wanted was to turn out like she had.

I spent a lot of time choosing what to wear on the first day of school, so I was the last one out the door, besides Mom. She wished me good luck as I grabbed two pieces of cinnamon toast, some bacon, and a banana from the kitchen table. Shouldering my new purple backpack, I coolly strolled off toward the middle school.

I put the bacon between the two slices of toast and crunched into it. It was a good thing I was outside because the crumbs flew everywhere.

It seemed so long ago that I had walked these sidewalks and passed these houses with Elaine when I was in kindergarten. I always had to run to keep up with her. One time she was mad because Mom had wanted Elaine to keep her hair out of her face. Finally she said that if Elaine didn't take care of it, she'd just have to get a haircut. Elaine stormed out the door. All the way to school, she complained about Mom and Dad. "Don't you just want to get away from them?" she fumed.

"No," I said.

"Oh, I forgot. You're the *good* one." Then she told me how much she didn't like me. I was in tears by the time we got to the playground. All she did was smile and tell the playground teacher I didn't want to go to school.

Why was Elaine such a rotten person? She did whatever she felt like doing and didn't care if she hurt other people. She took her problems out on everyone else.

One time Elaine had wanted to go to the lake with a bunch of friends, but Mom said no because she didn't know who the friends were. They argued about it, and Elaine left anyway. When Dad came home, Mom told him what had happened, and they left me with Brian while they drove off to get her back. Finally they came home and reported her missing to the police. An officer came over and filled out a report but said she was probably just out with her friends and would come home later. Mom and Dad were worried to death.

I fell asleep over my homework. Bumping noises from the living room woke me up. I peeked around my bedroom door to see Elaine trying to turn off the lamp in the living room. She leaned on a chair and stretched over it to turn off the lamp but burned her finger on the light bulb instead. She said a swear-word and stuck her finger in her mouth.

Suddenly Dad was up and out there. Mom followed behind, tying her robe around her waist.

"Where were you?" he asked. His voice had a furious, brittle edge to it. I was afraid that if Elaine smarted off, like she was bound to do, there was no telling what might happen.

"What's it to you?" Elaine slurred around her finger at him. She popped her finger out of her mouth and worked her way around the back of the chair. She needed both hands to hang on. She tried to weave her way past Dad, but he put both hands on her shoulders.

"You're my daughter," he said firmly.

Elaine tried to look off to the side, but he put his hand under her chin. "Where have you been?"

She made no answer.

He tugged on her chin. His voice grew louder as he spoke. "We didn't know if you'd come home or if we'd get a call from the police."

"You mean I had a choice?" It was hard for her to get the words out because of the way he was holding her chin.

"You listen to me!" he shouted. "I don't get up and go to work every morning so I can support somebody who goes out and does God knows what. You obey our rules. If you want to go out and get trashed, you had better wait until there's nothing I can do about it."

"There's nothing you can do about it now," Elaine said belligerently.

Dad leaned very close to her face. His words came out in such a low tone, and so quickly, that I had a hard time hearing them.

"There's nothing I *can't* do," he growled. "If I have to get the phone book and look up a drug and alcohol treatment program, you will go to the first listing I find. If you need a counselor, you will get the first one I find. If you need a hospital program, you will get into the first one I find. You name for me *one thing* I cannot do for you."

Elaine pulled her chin out of his grasp. "You can't make me happy," she said. That should have pushed Dad over the edge, but she sounded so sad that he didn't know what to say.

Mom put both hands over her mouth. The room was silent.

Dad took a breath and let it out very slowly. "I will do whatever is in my power," he said. "If you need help, I will find it."

"You can't help me," she said softly. She looked off to the side and shook her head. "There's nothing you can do. You don't understand." She sobbed like a child, loudly and painfully. Dad held her tightly.

"Understand what?" Dad pleaded.

She sobbed in his arms and shook her head.

Mom moved forward and took her gently by the shoulders. She put her arm around Elaine as they walked to the hallway.

I hid as they passed my door. As they went into Elaine's room, Mom soothed her. "We'll talk about it tomorrow. Right now you need some sleep."

"I'll sleep when I'm dead." Elaine sobbed.

"You don't mean that," Mom said and closed the door behind them.

I peeked into the living room again. Dad stood with his back to me, his head down. It almost looked as if he was praying. Like a tired old man, he walked to the lamp and turned it off. He shuffled his feet through the darkness back to his bedroom.

I went back to bed and fell asleep waiting for Mom to come out of Elaine's room. When my alarm went off the next morning, I tiptoed across the hall and carefully opened the door.

Elaine was curled up on her side under the covers, breathing deeply. Her eyes were closed. Her skin looked a little pink, and she was sleeping. It was the most peaceful I had ever seen her.

Mom was propped up beside her. She was pale but kept her eyes on Elaine, stroking her hair in rhythm with her breathing. When she finally noticed that I was watching, she took her hand off Elaine's head and put a finger to her lips.

I PROMISED MYSELF THAT I WOULD NOT BE LIKE THAT. IF there was a problem, I would take care of it myself. This was the first day of a new school year, a new chance.

Chapter 8

SIXTH GRADE WAS ALL RIGHT AT FIRST. CLASSES WEREN'T that hard, except for math, and I volunteered to work in the library on my study period.

But trouble came looking for me soon enough. Mr. Pope was my social studies teacher. New teachers are always easy to spot. They try to be popular with the students but then overdo it when there's a problem in class.

So there was Mr. Pope one day, talking about anthropology. He called on Greg Fischer to read a paragraph about Dr. Louis Leakey. Everybody knew that Greg was an excellent soccer player, but he couldn't read. He fidgeted and mispronounced words all over the place. It was awful to hear him stumble through the paragraph. We all shifted in our seats and waited for it to be over.

A commercial popped into my head. I flashed back to the time when Elaine wanted to go to the mall and Mom said O.K.—as long as I got to go with her.

I LOVED THE MALL, BUT ELAINE HADN'T WANTED TO TAKE me because she was meeting friends there. Mom had insisted that we go together, though, so she packed us off with ten dollars each and dropped us off by the J.C. Penney.

Elaine and her friends strolled from store to store, looking cool and making sure everyone heard them talking. When I tried to keep up, they ignored me, so I ended up trailing along behind them.

I stopped at the pretzel stand and got a soda. Then the pretzels looked good, so I bought one, too. When I looked around, Elaine and her friends were gone.

I sat down on a bench and ate, certain that they would come back looking for me. I ate slowly but was still alone when the food and drink were finished.

I looked at the passing strangers. Elaine and her friends weren't anywhere. Swallowing the fear in my throat, I threw out my trash and went back to the pretzel stand, whispering my telephone number to myself.

"Where's the phone?" I politely asked the lady.

"What do you need a phone for, honey?"

"I need to call home." It was a struggle to keep my voice from shaking. I wondered if I really did know my phone number.

"What's the matter?" She leaned over the counter and looked down at me.

"I came here with my sister, and now I can't find her." My voice cracked, and I began to cry.

People close by turned to look at me. They just felt sorry for a lost little kid, but I didn't want to be that kid. I hid my face in my hands.

"Here, honey," she said. I looked up to see her holding out several paper napkins. "Dry your eyes. We'll find your sister."

"Thank you." I tried to be delicate about blowing my nose.

A security guard passed by.

"John," she called out, "this little girl has lost her sister. Can you help her out?"

He scared me. His uniform made him look like a policeman. He knelt down so that our eyes met, and I could tell that he was friendly, but I backed up a step just the same.

“That sure is a pretty flowered shirt you have on,” he said. “What’s your name?”

I looked down at my pretty flowered shirt. No words came out of my mouth.

“You want to take a walk with me to the customer service desk?”

I looked up into his big, round face. He had dark brown eyes. “Am I in trouble?”

He laughed and shook his head. “No, sweetheart. We can call for your sister over the loudspeaker. She’ll hear us and come pick you up.”

I considered what he said. Mom and Dad had always told me not to go with strangers. I looked at the pretzel lady. “It’s O.K., honey. I know John real well,” she said.

John stuck out his big, strong hand, and I took it and started walking with him.

Strangers were all around us. As I looked up at their faces, I saw Elaine holding a bag. Her friends were with her. I tugged on John’s hand. “There’s my sister.” I pointed at Elaine, who smiled and waved at me.

He let go of my hand, and I walked over to Elaine.

“Get a little lost?” she asked innocently. Her friends giggled into their hands.

"We really missed you," said one.

"We looked all over," said the other.

I was boiling mad. I kicked Elaine so hard in the shin that she dropped her bag.

"Ow!" she yelled. She grabbed my arm. "If you had kept up with us, you wouldn't have gotten lost! You're so stupid!"

I kicked out and got the other shin. "Maybe you walk TOO FAST!" I yelled. "Maybe now you'll WALK SLOWER!"

Some of the people who were watching had started to laugh, but then Elaine leaned down and slapped my face, hard. "I didn't want you to come anyway!" she shouted. "I wish you were dead!"

"Hey!" John stepped in and took me by the hand and Elaine by the arm. "Don't you treat her that way." With people staring, he took us to customer service and handed us over to the chief security officer. He asked Elaine for our phone number, but she wouldn't tell him. I finally told him myself.

My face stung where she'd slapped me. She had wished me dead. I was too hurt to cry about it. I just wrapped my arms around my middle and felt sick.

Mom was really mad when she came to pick us up. She let me ride in front. Elaine sat behind me and kicked the back of my seat. She got grounded for a week and had to apologize for not watching me. She said she was sorry, but I didn't believe her.

I SHOOK MY HEAD TO CLEAR AWAY THE COMMERCIAL AND found myself staring right at the pointed tip of Mr. Pope's maroon tie. He braced his hands on the front corners of my desk and lowered his face close to mine.

"Hello! Could you make heads or tails out of that?" he asked loudly.

I thought he must have been talking about a coin toss, so I said, "Heads," and shrugged.

Everybody laughed but Greg and Mr. Pope.

"Oh God," he said, "one kid can't read, and the other one can't hear." He left my desk and returned to the front of the room.

Then I figured it out. "Don't pick on Greg," I said. It was my own fault for not listening, so I couldn't complain about that.

Some kids said "Oooooooh," but most of the class went quiet.

Mr. Pope stared at me. He was the sort of person who was handsome only at a distance. The more I looked at him, the less I liked him.

"This is my class," he said, waving his arm over the students. "I can pick on anyone I want."

"Not for the wrong reason." I looked him square in the eye.

When the class said "Oooooooh" again and made smooching noises, he blew a fuse. "That's it, Beck." He stomped over to his desk and yanked a small piece of paper out of the top drawer. He wrote on it furiously and then held it out in my direction. "Go to the office."

Suddenly I became stubborn. "My name's not Beck."

"Your last name is Beck. And you've got an office detention."

"My first name is Gina. And if you send me to the office, I'll tell Mr. Smith exactly what happened."

The class paid careful attention to us.

"Do you think he's going to believe you?" he asked. "Is he going to believe the smart mouth who got in trouble or the teacher who turned her in?"

"He's going to believe me," I said bravely, "because I'm going to tell him about it first." I gathered my things, snatched the detention slip from him, and walked righteously to the door, glimpsing the open mouths and wide eyes of the other students.

My legs trembled as I walked down the hall, but I told myself that I had done the right thing—even if it did get me kicked out. It was wrong of Mr. Pope to make fun of Greg's poor reading.

Mr. Smith's office was downstairs. I gave the detention slip to Miss Lemp, his secretary, and she politely asked me to sit down and said that Mr. Smith would meet with me soon. After a few minutes, Mr. Smith's door swung open, and Mrs. Jeffries, the principal, brushed past me. I looked up at her as she passed, but she only stared straight ahead. Then Miss Lemp took Mr. Pope's detention slip into Mr. Smith's office. They came out together.

Mr. Smith looked serious, but he held out his hand for me to shake and said, "I'm sorry we meet this way, Miss Beck."

I wiped my sweaty hand on my jeans and shook hands with him but didn't know what to say. His dark blue suit and tie intimidated me. He showed me into his office and asked me to have a seat.

I told him everything—even the things I had said—and he was very understanding. He said that Mr. Pope was a new teacher and that it would take him awhile to learn how to deal with disruptions in class. He also said that I owed Mr. Pope reasonable behavior, even though I might disagree with some of the things he did. Then he told me to sit in the detention room with Mrs. Johnson for the rest of the class period. I thought Mr. Pope should have been right in there with me.

Mrs. Johnson was a big, beautiful lady. Her skin was dark brown and shiny, like fine African wood. She wore brightly colored, flowing dresses. Her hair was just as curly and stubborn as mine. When she smiled she used her whole face, but her eyes remained calm and wise. Her voice was low and musical, like warm water running deep underground. She was a walking love poem. I could not figure out why in the world she worked there.

When the bell rang, I said good-bye to Mrs. Johnson and went to the library. I stashed my backpack under the counter and asked Mrs. Crane, the librarian, what she wanted me to do.

"Those books need to be checked in," she said pleasantly and pointed to a nearby cart. She was dressed predictably in a pale pink dress and cardigan sweater, and her hair was swept up in an ash-colored puff around her head. She was older and nerdy, but I liked her anyway.

I began to sort the books and match them with the check-out cards. I crossed off the name of the last person to have had the book and slipped the card into the book pocket. Then I had to organize the books on the cart and return them to the shelves.

The students assigned for study period came in. Some of them had come from Mr. Pope's class, and they waved at me as they passed.

Greg Fischer came in last. He walked to the counter and leaned over toward me. "It was really great the way you told off Mr. Pope," he said quietly.

I noticed his clear blue eyes and cropped blond hair. He smelled pleasantly of the spicy cologne that Brian wore sometimes. Suddenly he stood up straight, which forced me to look up at him. I realized that I had been staring and that he knew it.

"Well, it wasn't right," I stammered. I quickly looked at the book in my hands.

"Yeah," he said awkwardly.

I worked up the nerve to look him in the eye. "What was the assignment up there?"

He smiled. "Nothing. He totally lost it and just yelled at everybody until the bell rang."

"Cool!"

"I thought so." He turned and trotted out the door just before the tardy bell.

But it wasn't cool. It was stupid. Maybe I should have gone to Mr. Pope and apologized, but it was partly his fault, too. I decided to wait and see what would happen tomorrow.

As I returned a card to its pocket, I noticed Elaine's name on it toward the top. I gasped.

"Oh, Elaine," I whispered, examining the book, *The Little Prince.* It was a skinny little thing and obviously wasn't read by many people if the card was old enough to have her name on it. I set it aside.

After returning the books to the shelves, I checked out that little book for myself. I was relieved that I could do that without Mrs. Crane knowing about it.

I was glad to get home at the end of the day. I poured myself a glass of milk, grabbed a few raisin cookies, and headed off to my bedroom, where I stretched out on the bed and began reading. I became absorbed in the story and had just finished it when someone knocked softly on the door.

"Hey! Time for dinner," Brian called.

"Thanks," I called back, blinking my eyes in the dimness. I moved to turn on the lamp and almost knocked over the milk. It was warm, and the glass was beaded with moisture, so I took it back to the kitchen and poured the milk into the sink. I squinted in the bright light.

"Oh, you're home?" Dad asked me as he sat down to eat. "You've been quiet."

Telling everybody about my day might spoil dinner, so I said, "I was just reading a book."

Brian sat across from me, chewing thoughtfully. I showed him a skeleton smile and put my napkin in my lap.

"For homework?" Mom asked. She was bringing the rest of the meal to the table.

"No."

As Dad handed around the porkchops, he asked, "What's it about?"

I fished around with the corn and mashed potatoes before answering. "It's about a guy who crashes his airplane in the desert and meets a little boy from another planet."

"Science fiction?" asked Brian. He looked interested.

I shook my head. "Not really. I don't know what you'd call it."

"So, what happens?"

I swung my foot at him. "Read it yourself if you want to know."

"I felt that," Dad said.

"Oops. Sorry."

"Where did you find it?" Mom asked lightly.

I put down my fork. "Why don't you just ask me about what happened at school this afternoon?"

Mom and Dad looked at each other. "We thought you'd just bring it up," Dad said dryly.

So I told them what had happened. No one nagged at me for it, which was a relief. Mom and Dad gave me the speech about behaving in class whether I liked the teacher or not. They had told

Elaine that all the time, but they didn't need to tell me. I had no intention of repeating my visit to Mr. Smith's office. Soon we went back to being a normal family eating dinner. I was glad we weren't talking about the book anymore.

LATER, BRIAN SURPRISED ME, STOPPING BY MY ROOM TO get the book.

"It's on the bed," I said from my desk, where I was working on math. Mrs. "Hideous" Higgins had assigned an awful lot of homework.

He peered over my shoulder at what little I had done. "Ah, the Hideous One lives."

"You had her, too?"

"I think Moses had her."

"Maybe that's why he got lost in the desert. Who can understand her?" I stabbed my pencil at the paper.

"Look," he said kindly. "See this problem?" He pointed to $a \times 3 = 18$.

I nodded. "The answer is six. I know that. But Mrs. Higgins wants us to solve it *algebraically*." I imitated her high-pitched, nasal voice.

He imitated her as well, saying, "I can show you how to solve it *algebraically*." Then his voice returned to normal. "See the times sign in front of the three?"

"Yeah."

"If you're going to show how to solve this problem, you have to undo the multiplication."

"What?"

"Division undoes multiplication. Multiplication undoes division. So you take your three, there"—he stole my pencil and lightly circled the three and the multiplication sign—"and the times sign, and you undo it. Then you write the division sign and a three with it on the other side of the equation, after the eighteen. Then go back and cross out the times three." He demonstrated.

I frowned. "But she didn't do it that way."

"I'm showing you a shortcut. You're smart enough to do that. See? You're left with *a* by itself on one side of the equal sign, and now you have eighteen divided by three on the other side, so you get six for your answer."

"Oh!" I said. It looked easy now. Maybe I was smart enough to do it.

"See? It's a game. You have to know the rules in order to play. You just undo the sign, keep it with the number, and move them to the other side of the equation." He stood up.

"I get it! Thanks!"

He knuckle-rubbed my head, and I gave him a

monkey bite behind the knee. He told me that addition undoes subtraction, and subtraction undoes addition. Then he left with *The Little Prince*. Remembering the raisin cookies, I chewed them confidently and finished all fifty problems.

Chapter 9

I TOOK MY SEAT IN MR. POPE'S CLASS THE NEXT DAY. SOME people smiled at me, but I ignored them and got out my notebook.

When the bell rang, Mr. Pope called out, "Pop quiz!"

Everyone groaned.

"Get out a piece of paper and close your books. There will be ten questions." We scrambled to follow his orders. "Question one: Who was the leader of China during World War II?" He paced the room, watching us closely.

We had never talked about anybody in China. Glancing over at Mary Ann's paper, I saw that hers, like mine, was blank.

"Beck!" Mr. Pope called out angrily. "Get out!" He strode to my desk and slapped a detention slip on top of my paper.

I was shocked. Looking down at it, I asked, "What did I do?"

"You cheated during a quiz." He walked to the front of the class and stood there with his arms crossed.

Barbara laughed, but it was a mean laugh.

I WAS SUDDENLY REMINDED OF THIRD GRADE, WHEN THE other kids had told me that they wanted to sit by me because I was smart. I think the only reason they wanted to sit by me was to copy my work. But I went along with it because otherwise they might not be friends with me.

After a while I got tired of it. I misspelled a few words on a practice spelling test. Barbara misspelled them, too. Soon our teacher, Miss Malone, asked to talk to us in the hall.

She began by handing us our tests. I didn't need to look at Barbara's paper, but she sure looked over at mine. Her face turned red.

"Barbara, look at me," Miss Malone said quietly.

Tears fell on Barbara's paper, but she looked up at her.

"Your spelling test looks exactly like Gina's. Can you explain why that is?" Miss Malone bent down and looked closely at her.

"I don't know," Barbara said lamely.

Miss Malone straightened up to look down at me. "What do you know about this?" she asked in the same quiet tone.

She had dark brown eyes. I didn't like her eyes because it was hard to tell what she was thinking. They didn't give me any clue as to how this was going to turn out. I thought Barbara would be on the spot, not me.

"I did it on purpose," I said, dropping my head and looking at the floor. Suddenly I wished I had just said something to Barbara myself. Maybe that would have stopped it. I didn't like feeling this way.

"Did what on purpose?" Miss Malone asked in that deadly calm voice. She was very angry, but I didn't know how to stop what was happening. When Mom and Dad got mad at me, they yelled and raised a fuss. Miss Malone should have just yelled at me and gotten it over with. My face grew hot.

Stinging tears splashed down onto my paper. I was angry that Miss Malone could make me feel that

I had done something wrong when I hadn't. Words circled in my head like birds waiting to land, but I wouldn't speak. I wasn't sure how Miss Malone was going to react.

"What did you do on purpose?" Miss Malone asked me. She shifted her weight to her other foot and crossed her arms in front of her chest.

I shrugged but couldn't look at her. I didn't like to be made to cry.

Miss Malone took a step back and looked at both of us. "Well, let me tell you what I think. Gina, you get good spelling grades. Barbara, you don't do that well. When Barbara starts sitting by Gina, suddenly Barbara's grades improve. Do you know what that shows me? That shows me that Barbara is probably cheating. Is that true?"

Barbara nodded but didn't say anything.

"And what does Gina misspelling words tell me about Gina?"

I wasn't sure what she meant. Did Miss Malone think it was my fault that Barbara copied? If I wanted to miss a few words on the practice test, that was my business.

"That tells me that Gina doesn't want Barbara to copy from her. Gina, go ahead and tell Barbara that you don't want her to copy from you."

How much worse did she want to make it?

Miss Malone was searching for an answer in my mismatched eyes. My left eye looks sparkly blue because there are fine white streaks running from the pupil outward. Both of Brian's eyes are like that. My right eye is sort of a gray-blue color, like the sky on a cloudy autumn day. She looked first at my left eye, then at my right, and suddenly it seemed like maybe there were two different sides to me, and she was trying to get one of them to do what she wanted. I only had one mouth, thank goodness, and it stayed shut.

Miss Malone let a few terribly long minutes pass, then sighed through her nose. "All right," she said. She looked at Barbara, who had quit crying and was wiping her nose with the back of her hand. "Barbara, quit copying from Gina. She doesn't like it. Understood?"

Barbara nodded again.

"When we go back in the room, I will trade your desk with Randy's. That will be the end of that."

We went back to class. Everybody heard what had happened because Miss Malone had left the door open. I took my seat and put my head down on my desk, angry that she had made me feel guilty. I never meant for Barbara to be embarrassed for not being a good speller. I should have just talked to her myself.

I SNAPPED BACK TO THE PRESENT. BARBARA HAD CHEATED in third grade, but I knew that I hadn't cheated on Mr. Pope's quiz.

"There's nobody to cheat from. Nobody knows the answer." A whisper of agreement came from the class.

"Everybody would have known the answer if you hadn't disrupted class yesterday." His words were smug, but he squeezed his arms tightly as if he wasn't all that sure of himself.

I looked at Greg Fischer. He shrugged his shoulders and shook his head.

"Do you mean you're mad at everybody because you kicked me out?" My heart jittered. I didn't want to argue with him, but he wasn't making any sense.

Mr. Pope frowned. He walked to the intercom and placed his hand on the call button. "I will have you escorted from this room," he said.

"I didn't do anything wrong," I protested.

We stared at each other. The class shifted nervously in their seats. Finally, he crossed over to his desk at the front of the room and shouted out nine more questions. Of course, no one knew the answers.

"Pass your papers forward." He made a big deal of looking over the blank sheets. "No one passed the quiz," he announced. "I would have been willing to throw it out, but because of Beck's behavior, I'm forced to make a point. Everyone receives an F for their daily grade today. If this upsets you, I suggest you talk to her about it."

The class gasped and muttered. Mr. Pope sat at his desk and did paperwork for the rest of the period without speaking to us.

When the bell rang, everyone else left in a hurry, but I headed up to his desk.

"That wasn't fair," I said angrily.

"Lots of things aren't fair," he replied, writing zeroes in the grade book. He didn't look up at me.

"Don't take it out on everybody else if you're mad at me."

He was silent.

It was a waste of time. As I turned to leave, he called out, "Don't bother coming back tomorrow, Beck. You've got another office detention."

"My *name* is Gina," I said and slammed the door behind me.

I went to Mr. Smith's office the next afternoon during social studies class and told him everything. He asked me a few questions and looked concerned. Then he asked me to spend the rest of the period in the detention room with Mrs. Johnson.

I was slaving over the math assignment from that morning when I heard voices in the front office. After a few minutes, Mr. Smith escorted Greg Fischer into the room and introduced him to Mrs. Johnson.

She seated Greg at the opposite end of the room from me, which wasn't too far because there was only room for ten desks, including the big one that Mrs. Johnson used. While Mr. Smith and Mrs. Johnson whispered, Greg and I looked at each other and shrugged.

After Mr. Smith left, I started on my math again but couldn't remember how Mrs. Higgins had told us to do it. As I sat scowling, I heard Greg ask, "Mrs. Johnson?"

"Yes?" came the warm voice.

"Could I help Gina with her homework?"

Her words washed over the room. "You sit and work silently. You're in here for a reason."

Greg looked at me and shrugged. He opened his backpack and began to work on the English assignment. I watched his lips move as he read. I looked up at Mrs. Johnson, who was watching both of us.

"Mrs. Johnson?" I asked, trying to keep my voice as pretty as hers.

"Go ahead," she said quietly. "But if there's any playing around, I'm putting an end to it."

"We won't." I moved next to him, feeling both shy and very conscious of the heavy math book I dragged with me. He just sat and stared. I had known him ever since he smacked me in the face with a kickball in fourth grade, but I had never felt especially kindly toward him. I settled in and pulled his book over so I could see it better. Remembering how Brian had helped me, I took it one step at a time. "O.K., we've got subjects and predicates. The subject tells what we're talking about. The predicate tells what happened."

Greg blinked at me. "What?"

"You're smart enough to do this," I said calmly, trying to do what Brian would have done to get him to follow along. "Listen, I'll read first, then you read, then you tell me the subject and the predicate. Look, I'll show you."

It took him a few minutes, but he ended up doing pretty well. Sometimes he misread a word, but he corrected himself, and he always knew where the subject and predicate were. If he could hear it, he could do it. We got through his homework, and he was showing me how to do my math when the bell rang.

We jumped. I returned to my desk and packed my things. Greg was out of there like a shot. As I passed Mrs. Johnson, she smiled deeply and winked.

I returned the smile but couldn't figure out what the wink was about.

Chapter 10

BRIAN CHECKED OVER MY MATH THAT NIGHT. I HAD WANTED to talk to him about Mr. Pope but changed my mind. I'd just have to work it out by myself.

"Looks good to me," he said and handed back my paper. "Here," he said, getting Elaine's book from his desk.

I took it from him. "What did you think?"

"The little boy was kind of desperate. I think it shows that people will go to any length to protect what they love," he said sadly.

"Yeah, right," I said bitterly. "What did Elaine ever love?"

"You, for one thing."

I almost dropped my math paper. "You've got to be kidding!" How many times had she wished me dead or called me stupid? I didn't know what was precious to her, but it couldn't have been me.

"Yeah, she picked on you all the time. But that's because you're the little sister. I picked on her because she was my little sister."

"But you never said the things she did."

Brian shrugged. "She had a mean streak in her; I won't deny that. But do you remember who taught you to read?"

I shook my head.

"One guess."

"Huh. No way."

He nodded. "I remember her sitting with you on her lap at the kitchen table while she read to you. She pointed to each word and made you say it after she did."

I shook my head. "I don't remember that."

"You were little, maybe four. It was before you went to school."

I stood there and tried to recall. Finally I shook my head. "That's not really protecting me."

He raised his eyebrows. "Do you remember us taking you to the playground?"

"A few times."

"One time there was this kid who was throwing rocks at you while you were on the swings. I yelled at him, but before I could get over there, Elaine had jumped off the monkey bars and pushed him down." He smiled a little. "She wanted to beat him up. I had to pull her off him."

Brian had had to pull her off me plenty of times.

"What happened?"

"Oh, he got up and ran off. He said he was going to get his dad."

"Did he?"

"Nah. I said to go ahead and bring him on. We waited for a little while, but nobody showed up."

"What would you have done if he'd shown up?"

Brian laughed. "I told Elaine I would beat up his dad and she could beat up the kid."

I smiled. "Where was I?"

"Still swinging. You were up too high and couldn't slow down for a while."

"I wish I remembered that."

He shrugged. "Elaine didn't start out that bad. I think that as she got older, she developed some problems."

I looked down at the book. "What else did she love?"

He took a few breaths, then quietly said, "I don't know. Herself, I guess. I think she protected herself by being mean."

I looked at him. "Why?"

"Well, think about it. If you're mean as a dog, nobody gets near you. They don't get to see your weaknesses."

"Yeah, and they also don't get a chance to like you," I said bitterly. I took my homework back to my room and thought about what he had said.

A few days later, while Mom was grocery shopping and Brian and Dad were working in the yard, I went into Elaine's room again. It was still a jumbled mess, which reminded me of the laundry incident.

ELAINE HAD BEEN REALLY MAD BECAUSE SHE WAS RUNNING out of clean clothes. She'd screamed and yelled at Mom, who'd shrugged and told her to do her own wash if those album covers were still on the wall. She pitched a fit and threw her clothes into the hallway. Some landed in my room. I picked them up and put them in my hamper. Mom did the laundry later and gave them back to me! At first, I was going to return them to Elaine, but she would have just yelled at me anyway, so I decided to keep them.

She had some cool stuff! I ended up with an emerald green sweatshirt that was much too big, a pair of jeans, a blue flannel shirt, and a great big white sweatshirt that ballooned out like a tent and hung below my knees. Of course I didn't wear those things when she was around, and, besides, they didn't even fit. But I kept them in my closet anyway.

The laundry pile grew in the hallway. Elaine didn't pick it up until Dad said that if she didn't, he was going to get a trash bag and throw it all out. When I came home from school one afternoon, the mess was gone and so was Elaine. After dark a car pulled into the driveway, and Elaine came to the front door with a lady wearing a dark green sweatsuit. Brian and I were watching television in the living room and saw everything that happened.

They each carried in a full basket of clean clothes. While Elaine went into her room and unpacked hers, this lady started to tell Mom off.

"Elaine is a student and shouldn't be expected to have to do her own wash. How do you think she feels when she has to wear dirty clothes to school?" she asked. Her hair was dyed red, and she smelled like cigarette smoke. Elaine smiled at Mom when she took the second basket from the lady's arms.

Mom held her chin up and said, "I tell my daughter to do her own wash when she refuses to take down distasteful things from her bedroom walls and forbids me to enter her room. Perhaps you'd like to take a little tour and see things for yourself. Oh, Elaine," she called over her shoulder. Elaine was coming back with the empty baskets. "Perhaps you'd like to show this nice lady that dump you call a bedroom. Maybe you'd like to tell her the real story behind your laundry and why it hasn't been done."

Elaine swept past both of them as they stood in the doorway. She returned with a third basket. She said nothing as she hurried to her bedroom. The red-haired lady stuck out her right hand and said, "I'm Franny Greco, Diana's mother. I'm really sorry. Guess I stuck my nose in where it didn't belong."

Mom shook Franny Greco's hand firmly. "You certainly did, Ms. Greco. But Elaine can be manipulative," she said.

"She's a very convincing person."

"Yep," said Mom and crossed her arms. She stared solidly at Ms. Greco until Elaine came back with the last empty basket.

"Thank you, Franny," she said sweetly as she handed it over.

Ms. Greco looked at Mom and then spoke to Elaine. "You made a fool out of me."

Elaine crossed her arms. Her lips firmed into a thin line, and her face moved from sunny and sweet to dark and angry.

Mom looked at Elaine. "This little stunt is going to cost you—oh, what would you say, Ms. Greco? Ten dollars? Does that cover your time and expenses?"

"It's fair."

Elaine rolled her eyes and glared at Mom.

"Pay the lady," said Mom. "And call her Ms. Greco, please."

Ms. Greco casually waved her hand. "Oh, all the kids call me Franny."

"I don't have it," Elaine snapped.

"You have twenty-five dollars in your money jar."

"You said you'd stay out of my room!"

Mom shrugged. "You didn't keep it clean, so I didn't stay out of it."

"You snooped through my things!" Elaine stomped her foot.

"Yes, and it took forever. I'm surprised you can find anything in there. Now go wade through that mess and bring back ten dollars for Ms. Greco. Quick!"

"Franny," said Ms. Greco.

Mom turned to her and arched an eyebrow. "Ms. Greco," she said firmly.

Elaine snarled as she stalked off to her room and slammed the door shut. It burst open a few minutes later, and she came back with the money. She threw it down on the floor and turned to leave, but Mom caught her by the sweatshirt hood. Elaine almost fell over backward. Mom pulled back on the hood until Elaine was eye to eye with her.

"Stop it! You're wrecking my shirt!"

"I'll finish the job unless you pick up that money and hand it gently to Ms. Greco," Mom said calmly. "You also owe her an apology."

They glared at each other. Elaine was just a little taller than Mom, and I thought there was going to be a fight. Elaine tried to take a step forward, but Mom held her ground.

Suddenly, Elaine turned, scooped up the ten dollars, and flung it at Ms. Greco, who barely caught it before Elaine broke free and fled to her room. She slammed the door so hard that it made the pictures jump on the wall.

"Elaine!" Mom shouted.

"What?" she shouted back from the bedroom.

"Your apology!" Mom crossed her arms again and looked calmly at Ms. Greco.

I thought I heard a few swearwords, and then she screamed, "SORRY!"

"Ms. Greco!" Mom continued.

Something hit the wall in Elaine's bedroom, and then we heard, "Ms. Greco!"

Brian and I clapped our hands over our mouths to keep from laughing out loud. We rolled our eyes at each other and struggled to keep quiet.

Ms. Greco shook her head sympathetically. "Oh, you've got your hands full." She held out the ten dollars. "I don't need this, Mrs. Beck. Go buy yourself some aspirin with it."

Mom shook her head and allowed herself a small smile. "I won't let her off the hook. She owes you that money."

They wished each other a good night. Then Mom calmly closed the front door, walked to Elaine's room, and opened the door.

"Stay *out* of my room!" Elaine screamed at her.

The door clicked shut. We could hear shouting and screaming from Elaine and the sounds of things getting smashed. We could also hear Mom's voice—not as loud as Elaine's, but deadly firm. Then the door opened and Mom called, "Gina?"

Brian and I, who had almost burst out laughing, straightened up.

"Yes?" I called back from the living room. I half expected her to ask for an ambulance.

"Please get me some trash bags from under the kitchen sink. Three bags." Her voice was a little rough.

"Body bags," Brian whispered.

I jumped up and got the bags. My hands shook as I tore them from the box. They were slippery, which didn't make it any easier. Excited and scared, I rushed past Brian to Elaine's door. Mom stood with her back to me. Peeking around her, I saw that the walls were bare. The desk lamp was broken, along with a glass puppy I had given Elaine as a present. The album covers were torn to pieces and scattered all over the floor. Then I saw Elaine sitting way back on her bed, scowling at Mom.

"Get your *ugly face* out of here!" she shrieked at me.

I didn't dare laugh at her. I held out the bags until Mom could feel them touch her hand. "Thank you, Gina," she said as she let them slip to the floor. "My dear," she hissed to Elaine, "you get all of this *trash* put in these *bags* and get them out to the garbage cans before your *father* gets home. If I don't see three bags of *trash* out there before then, I'll come in here and finish the job myself. And if I do that, you'll have *very* few things left in this *room*."

I backed up quickly so that she wouldn't step on me as she quietly closed the door. Her face was red. I had never seen her so angry.

When Dad came home, he complained about the three extra trash bags by the garbage cans. Mom told him to just *be quiet*.

THOSE IMAGES TUGGED AT ME NOW, BUT I PUSHED THEM aside. This time I wanted something different.

Without thinking, I unsquashed the pillow and made the bed. At her desk, I gathered the stray pens and pencils and returned them to the holder.

The top desk drawer was an awful jumble of junk and writing supplies. There were pennies and phone numbers mixed with erasers and paper clips. Her silver bell earrings were stuffed way in the back. I held them up and listened to them jingle. They were finely made but a little tarnished. I put them gently in her jewelry box.

I pretended she was glad I was cleaning things up. It was my thanks for those few times when she'd showed that she loved me—the times Brian had told me about.

"Gina?"

I jumped and dropped the lid of Elaine's jewelry box. I spun around to see Mom at the door. She was staring at the bed.

"What are you doing?" she gasped.

"Cleaning," I said weakly.

She just stood there and looked around the room.

"Don't be mad," I begged.

"I'm not." She sighed and sat down on the bed.

I sat down beside her. "I just wanted to do something."

She nodded.

"Why was she so mean to me?"

She took a deep breath. "I don't know. She had a hard time with a lot of things. She didn't understand that she couldn't do whatever she wanted. She fought against us."

She could see that I didn't really understand. She rubbed at her nose and asked, "Remember the night you watched her come home? When Dad told Elaine there was nothing he couldn't do for her?"

My eyes widened.

"You had to have heard the whole thing," Mom said candidly. "Anyway, your father and I tried to make appointments for her, but she refused to go. She said she didn't have a problem."

Typical Elaine! "Mom, that's not true." I took her hand. "She was a real pain in the rear sometimes."

She smiled sadly. "What I wouldn't give to have that pain in the rear back. It's hard to lose a child, Gina," she said carefully. "As a parent, you're not finished with that child yet, and that child isn't finished with you. Everything's left undone. You've got bits and pieces of someone you'd hoped would become a complete adult."

I sort of knew what she was talking about. There was a lot about Elaine that didn't add up.

Mom looked around. "Someday we'll clear this out. But I'm just not ready yet. I need to come in here and think sometimes."

I nodded.

She stood up. "Anyway," she said briskly, "I came to tell you that the guys are doing the barbecue dance around the grill. Why don't you help me get the rest of lunch ready?"

"All right."

She put her arm around my shoulder and led me out of the room. "It will take time to sort this out. You can't just fold up a person and put her away."

I guess not.

Chapter 11

Monday was better. I guess Mr. Pope had decided to ignore me, because he wouldn't call on me during class discussion. I didn't need to please him, anyway, but it was still weird.

Everyone thought Greg Fischer and I were an item. It was embarrassing because we were just friends. But every time I looked up at him, he was just turning his head away.

"He's cute," said Mary Ann.

"I hardly think so," I said and felt my face buzz.

"Uh-huh," Mary Ann said and smiled at me.

It drove Tracy crazy. She sat right behind him and kept sticking her feet under his chair. When he'd accidentally kick her foot, she'd say, "Ow, Greg, that hurts!" and smile. He ignored her.

That day she poked him in the back with her pen. She didn't make marks, but he leaned forward every time she did it. She giggled. When she saw that I was watching, she gave me this really nasty look, which made me smile. I wasn't jealous of her. It looked like Greg had a little friend.

After the assignment was given and we were all working on it, Greg looked over at me. He pointed to his book and shrugged. I jerked my pen over toward his desk and shrugged back.

The bell rang. "Hand in your assignments," said Mr. Pope.

"I'm not done yet," said Blake, who looked shocked. He had never turned in an incomplete assignment before.

"I want to grade what you've done in class."

Mr. Pope stood by the door and dismissed us individually. He looked over each student's work, and if he was satisfied, he let the student go. It was getting late in the passing period. Those of us who were still sitting would probably be late for the next class. Finally, there were just three of us left: Greg, myself, and—guess who?—Tracy.

"You three stay after school today and finish this work," he said and walked back to his desk. He didn't even collect our papers.

"Do you want us to come back here?" I asked politely. Everybody knew that the teachers hung out in the lounge after school.

"Duh," he answered, rattling the papers on his desk.

Duh, I mouthed to Greg and Tracy. Greg smirked, but Tracy turned away. We gathered our things quickly and got out of there.

Greg stayed on my mind while I worked in the library. Why was that? We'd been in class together for years, and I'd never had much to say to him before. Maybe Tracy's jealousy had made things more interesting.

The three of us met in Mr. Pope's classroom after school.

"Let's go through his desk," said Tracy after we'd waited for Mr. Pope to arrive.

"Nah," said Greg as he took a seat at the study table in the back of the room. Of course Tracy had to sit right next to him. That was all right. I sat across from them. We wrestled our backpacks open.

I turned to the assignment and read out loud. We stopped to check the study questions and answered those if we could. I got nervous after a while, though, because Greg was staring at me—but only when he wasn't suddenly jerking in his chair. Tracy must have been kicking him under the table, because she'd move, and then he'd move. I heard him drag his feet across the floor. Tracy jerked one more time, and I heard her foot hit his chair. Soon we finished up and left our work on Mr. Pope's desk.

It was a beautiful September afternoon. The clear breeze was crisp with the rustle and scent of turning leaves. It was just warm enough to walk home with my jacket open. I wanted to walk behind Greg and Tracy, but they poked around too much—or rather, she did. I had better things to do besides compete for Greg's attention.

"See ya," I called, turning off a block early.

"I thought you went this way," he said and pointed ahead.

"Not today." I needed time to think.

I walked the rest of the way home and let myself into the house. I stood in front of Elaine's school picture in the living room. Pretending she was alive and in a good mood, I went into her room and sat on the bed. I whispered to her about Greg and imagined her laughter. The pretend Elaine asked me to tell her more and laughed again at my embarrassment.

What was I thinking? Of course she would have screamed at me to get out of there.

I decided that if he liked me, it was O.K. because I liked him, too. I liked helping him with his homework. He wasn't dumb.

I got up and looked into Elaine's mirror. "Thanks for listening," I said. "I appreciate it."

"No problem. Anytime," I answered myself.

I paused and considered my reflection. Something was different about my face. I couldn't quite tell what it was but finally decided that something was changing.

OF COURSE, MR. POPE DIDN'T FIND OUR WORK. HE HANDED back everyone else's papers and let them finish in class. We had to sit there and write "I will complete each daily assignment quickly and turn it in promptly to Mr. Pope" two hundred times.

"Do we get credit for it?" I asked.

He didn't answer me, so I knew that it was just a waste of our time.

He was making sure I would not get a good grade. Mr. Smith knew what was going on, but nothing happened. If Mom and Dad came to school about it, Mr. Pope would be sure to talk smoothly to them and then punish me later. I wasn't trying to be disrespectful, but he had caught me off guard with his surprise rules.

He collected our papers at the end of class. Instead of the sentence, I had written:

Mr. Pope,

I am trying very hard to get along with you. I want to do well, but you are making it impossible. Please try to get along with me.

Sincerely,

GINA Beck

WE DISCUSSED ARTIFACTS THE NEXT DAY. MR. POPE ASKED us to name some examples, and I said an arrowhead. He used my answer to ask where an arrowhead might be found.

"In the ground," said Denise.

"How would you find it in the ground?" asked Mr. Pope.

"You'd have to dig it up," Mary Ann said.

"If you dug up Gina's sister, you'd find a beer bottle with her," Tracy interrupted. "That would be an artifact." She turned and smirked at me.

My lungs slammed shut. The room was absolutely still. I looked at Mr. Pope.

"Just shut up, Tracy," muttered Greg.

I flashed back to that awful day in Mr. Swayze's class when Barbara had made that stupid comment about me and he had ignored it. I stared at Mr. Pope and hoped he would say something.

He cleared his throat. "Tracy, that was very rude. You owe Gina an apology."

Tracy shrugged and poked Greg in the back. He scooted his desk away from her. Everybody watched her turn pink and doodle busily in her notebook.

Mr. Pope cleared his throat again. "I'm sorry that Tracy was so rude to you, Gina."

I looked up and saw that he was sincere. I nodded my head and looked down at my notebook.

"Tracy? Is there no apology coming from you?" Mr. Pope walked to her desk and tried to look her in the eye.

She lowered her head and scribbled furiously, her pen shouting at the paper.

"Don't come back here tomorrow then. You'll have an appointment with Mr. Smith."

Tracy didn't respond, but her face turned a deeper red.

He turned away from her desk and assigned the class some work. When the bell rang, he let us go without collecting the assignment.

My feelings had come to a slow boil. Even if Tracy had apologized, it wouldn't have meant anything.

She had acted that way on purpose. I forced my homework into my backpack. As I rose from my seat, Mary Ann called out, "Hey, wait for me."

I stood there and took deep breaths, just like Dad does to calm himself.

"Don't pay any attention to her," she said and patted my shoulder. "She's just trying to get you mad. She wants to make you jealous."

"I'm not jealous of that little wet rag." My words trembled with anger.

"Don't let her get to you. She's being stupid," Mary Ann warned.

I nodded and tried to collect my feelings as we entered the hallway. An eerie calm hung in the air. People from my class kept away from me. The only ones in my way were Tracy and Greg. She was hanging on his sweatshirt sleeve.

He yanked his sleeve away from her. "Knock it off!" he said over his shoulder. "I'm sick of you bugging me all the time. Get away!" He stalked off down the hall.

Tracy stood still. I tried to walk around her, but she took a sudden step to her left and got in my way again. We bumped into each other.

She turned to face me. With a sickly sweet smile, she said, "Your sister's a dead drunk."

Those horrible words were the last straw. I punched her so fast that there wasn't time to think about it.

She cried out and sat down hard on the floor. I just stood there, my hand throbbing and my whole body shaking with rage.

Shouts of "Fight! Fight!" exploded in the air. Teachers swarmed out of their rooms. Mary Ann pulled me away from Tracy, who was now curled up in a ball.

"I'm not going to beat her up," I said tightly and pulled away from her. It was hard to keep myself together. I didn't know what to do next. All the noise and movement in the hallway just added to my confusion.

Suddenly someone came up behind me and yanked my arm back and to the side. I stumbled and bashed my forehead against the lockers. There was a sharp pain and then blood everywhere. Holding my hand against the cut, I turned to see Mr. McClure, whose classroom is down the hall from Mr. Pope's.

I burst into tears, not only because of my injury, but because all my emotions had been let loose inside. When I tried to pull free of him, he held on tighter and pulled me all the way to Mr. Smith's office.

Chapter 12

Mr. Smith decided to give me five days of in-school suspension. Then he looked at my forehead and decided to get the nurse. The nurse decided to call my mom, but I told her that Dad's office is closer. She tried to call him but found that he was gone at a conference and couldn't be reached. Finally she called the high school to get Brian to pick me up.

He rushed up in his beautiful old car and parked in the handicapped space. The principal, Mrs. Jeffries, told him that she was going to call the police to give him a parking ticket. He ignored her and got me out of there.

As we sped to the hospital, I held a thick wad of paper towels to my forehead. I was still crying, and the tears ran down onto my sweatshirt.

"Put your head back," he ordered. The towels were slick and hard to keep in place.

We went to the emergency room, where they made me lie down. A nurse rubbed orangey-yellow stuff on my forehead. It looked like mustard but smelled like chemicals. A doctor came in and numbed my skin with some lotion. Then I got six stitches. After a while, Brian came in and sat there with me but didn't say much.

"Fight at school?" the doctor asked casually.

"Yeah," I said, holding my head still.

"What does the other guy look like?"

"I don't know. I hit her in the eye."

"Did she give you this little paper cut?" asked the nurse.

"No. A teacher pulled on my arm, and I fell into the lockers."

Their mouths turned down and their eyebrows turned up, and they didn't ask me any more about it.

When they were through, they said I had to stay lying down. The nurse gave Brian some information sheets on head injuries and how to keep the stitches clean. They also gave him a note that I could take to school to excuse me from P.E. When he signed my release forms, the nurse at the desk didn't believe that he was eighteen and made him show his driver's license. She'd started to ask about insurance when the emergency-room doors slid open and Mom rushed in, her tense, high-heeled footsteps echoing off the walls.

"They told me you'd be here," she gasped as she made her way toward us. Her trench coat hung open and flapped behind her like a slate blue cape. She must have run her fingers through her hair the entire way to the hospital, because she looked like she'd just gotten out of bed. Her eyes were wide and moist, and she was breathing so quickly that I thought she'd pass out.

"Honey, are you all right?" She took me by the shoulders and examined my forehead. "How did it happen?"

"It's under control, Mom," Brian said and laid a hand on her shoulder. I started to tell Mom about the fight, but the nurse interrupted, saying that she needed insurance information. Brian and I waited while Mom talked to her.

We finally walked out the sliding doors and into the parking lot. I bunched my hands up inside my sweatshirt sleeves and wrapped my arms around my waist. My jacket was still at school. The autumn sky had turned from afternoon blue to sunset pink and purple. Suddenly I felt cold and shaky.

Mom wanted me to ride home with her, but Brian wasn't so sure. "If she barfs, my car would be a lot easier to clean out," he said. Mom had to agree with that. She had bought her pretty gold sedan with leather seats only last year. We walked over to her car. "Drive carefully, Mom," he said. "We'll be right behind you." We saw her off and then walked over to Brian's car.

He made me sit in the back on the way home. "You've already messed up the front," he said. "Good thing I can clean it up." I looked and saw smudges and swipes of browning stains on the front seat. My stomach churned. I slumped and rested my aching head, grateful that he turned on the heat full blast for me. As we drove home I told him what had been happening at school. I left Greg out of it.

"You can only take so much from people," he said. He tilted the rearview mirror so that he could see me. "But you can't let ignorant people get to you, even if they do something to you first."

We pulled into the driveway just after sunset. The leftover light was caught by wispy purple clouds fading away to jewel blue. I opened my door, but he told me not to get out until he came around to my side.

"It's not like I need an escort," I said.

"I don't want you to fall and break open some other part of your head. I have enough to take care of already." He gently took my arm and put his other hand on top of my head to shield it as I got out of the car. He held my arm as we went up the back steps.

Mom held the door open for us and took custody of me as we entered the kitchen. While Brian rummaged under the sink for cleaning supplies, Mom sat me down at the table, looked closely again at my stitches, and made me repeat the whole story.

When I was finished, she nodded and looked out the window. After a minute, she asked, "You didn't leave out anything?"

"No." I shook my head, feeling my brain slosh around. I held my head in both hands and rested my elbows on the table.

"You need to change that shirt," she said softly.

I looked down at myself. My dark green sweatshirt was streaked with blood, and it was beginning to smell. "It's ruined," I moaned.

Brian had finished with the car and was walking by with the cleaning supplies. He looked over and said, "Let me have it. It's not wrecked."

Mom gave him a weary but grateful look.

I went to my room and pulled Elaine's blue flannel shirt out of my closet. In the bathroom, I was shocked to see dried blood smeared on my pale face. I leaned closer to the mirror and looked at my forehead. It still had that yellow stuff from the hospital on it. The stitches were dark blue, and seeing the knots that held my skin together made me feel woozy. I hurried to get my sweatshirt off, easing it over my head. I pulled on the flannel, which felt like putting on a big warm hug. Then I tied my hair back and washed my face, careful to keep away from the stitches.

Dad had me tell the story again when he came home. We sat at the kitchen table while Mom and Brian got dinner ready. When I repeated what Tracy had said about Elaine, he flinched and crossed his arms.

"So, you've got five days in the detention room," he said.

Brian nodded. "The slammer," he said and smiled at me.

I wondered if he had ever been in there.

"The teacher should have thrown that girl out right away. She ought to get punished for what she said," Dad said, clearly upset.

"Well, she might have a black eye," I offered.

He smiled a little. "But you shouldn't have hit her. You'll have to pay the price for that, you know."

"Yeah." There was no way out of it.

"You probably should have talked to Mr. Smith."

I rolled my eyes. "Remember my problem with Mr. Pope?"

"Yes," Dad said, moving back from the table as Brian set out the plates.

"Well, every time I went to Mr. Smith, he listened and all that, but nothing ever changed."

"Why didn't you tell us?" Mom asked.

I shrugged. I was beginning to see how stupid it was to keep things to myself. "I wrote Mr. Pope a note about it."

"Did he talk to you?"

"No, but he was nicer to me." It felt like ages since the afternoon.

"There are a lot of jerks in this world," Dad said. "You can't just hit people because they get to you."

I didn't eat much dinner. Mom said that she would slice some of the roast and put a sandwich in the refrigerator for me. She checked my temperature, peered into my eyes, and sent me to bed early.

"But I'm not tired," I protested.

"You will be. We'll put the little TV in your room tonight."

There was no more to say about it, so I soon crawled into bed and propped my head on the pillows. I had just turned on the television when Brian knocked and asked to come in.

He'd saved my sweatshirt! It was folded up all nice and neat. He laid it on my desk.

"Thanks a lot," I said.

"Call me Laundry Man," he said in a deep voice and thumped his fist on his chest.

"Laundry Man, you're my hero," I said in a high voice and clasped my hands together.

He reached out and rapped my head.

"Ouch!" I swatted at his hand, but he pulled it away just in time.

He turned to leave, but before he could go I asked, "Did you ever get in a fight about Elaine?"

He came over and sat down on my bed. "I will never tell."

"That means you did."

He made the skeleton face.

I took a few breaths, then asked, "What kind of person was Elaine, really?"

He paused. "Does this have anything to do with that book you checked out?"

I shrugged.

He sighed. "I don't think she knew what kind of person she was. She didn't really get a chance to find out."

I nodded carefully.

"And don't drive yourself crazy looking in that book for clues." He grabbed a book from my shelf and held it up. "Could I figure out who you are by reading this?"

"No. It's not that great of a book anyway."

He put the book back. "That book was just something she read a long time ago. All the things she did and all the things she owned, that's just stuff. You know what she liked, but you have no evidence of who she was. You've got to let her go."

I pursed my lips.

"Some things will just never add up. You have to accept that."

I yawned.

He stood up and stretched. "Go to sleep, little Fruit. You've got a big detention tomorrow."

"Watch that Fruit stuff," I said. "Your forehead may be next."

"I doubt you're in the mood for a doubleheader."

He smiled and said good night, leaving my door open a bit. I tried to watch TV but fell asleep before the first commercial break.

Chapter 13

THE ALARM CLOCK BUZZED ME AWAKE. I WAS IN THE SAME spot where I had fallen asleep. The TV was off and the remote was on top, which meant that somebody had checked on me. I stretched, then gently touched my forehead. It still hurt, and I got out of bed wondering if my head would pound like it had last night. I only had a minor headache, but I still thought about faking it and staying home.

I yawned and walked to the full-length mirror hanging on the back of my door. When I turned on the light, I saw a hot, bluish purple lump spreading out in all directions from the wound. It sat right between my hairline and my eyebrows. I carefully touched it again. What a great-looking bruise! I changed my mind about missing school. This was too good to keep to myself.

I washed up and put on a red T-shirt. Red isn't my favorite color, but it complemented my forehead. Then I twisted my hair up and clipped it back. From prior experience, I knew that the detention room was a little warm—best not to overdress for the occasion.

Brian was standing at the sink when I rounded the corner in the kitchen. Dad had long ago given up on making him sit at the breakfast table with the rest of us. Brian was eating the sandwich that Mom had left in the fridge for me. "Hey, that's mine," I said.

Chewing noisily, he held it out and said around a mouthful of food, "Wanna bite?" He started to open his mouth, but I made a face and squinted my eyes shut.

"Nice mark," he said, waving the sandwich toward my head. "How do you feel?"

I yawned. "Not bad, I guess. I'm hungry. What's in here?" I opened the refrigerator to take a look.

"Step aside," ordered Mom as she came into the kitchen. She was dressed in her navy blue suit, and her heels tapped on the linoleum as she brushed me away. She peered into the fridge and pulled out eggs and bacon, bread, milk, juice, butter, and jelly. I hurried to find space on the counter as she thrust each item at me.

Not much later, I was seated at the table looking at a plate of scrambled eggs, which Mom said were good for me. She knew I hated them. I tried the hot pepper sauce on them while her back was turned.

"What are you doing?" asked Brian. He had finished the sandwich and was now working on a piece of bacon.

"Disguising this disgusting dish," I said. I sprinkled on more hot sauce, but too much came out. I decided to put it out with ketchup.

Dad came in and sat down. He filled his plate from the platters Mom had set on the table. He glanced over at my eggs and said, "Still bleeding?"

Brian laughed, then coughed on his mouthful of bacon. Mom looked over and asked, "What did you do?"

Wasn't it obvious? I bravely dug in and took a bite. My mouth burst into flames. I gulped the juice, but that didn't help. Finally, I pushed my plate away. "Can I do this over?"

Mom shook her head. "Just eat your breakfast. Hurry up."

After I choked it down with plenty of juice, Brian said, "You know, milk is a lot more effective on hot sauce."

"Now you tell me," I said, fanning my face. I squeezed a napkin over my nose.

"Hot sauce?" Mom asked, looking quizzically at us.

"Ah," Dad said and nodded. "By the way, some-one named Greg called for you last night."

"Oooh, Greggy Weggy," teased Brian and leaned back in his chair.

I glared at him.

He laughed and pointed at me. "Look at you!"

"All right, Brian," said Dad.

We finished up and headed out the door. It was a beautiful, clear cool morning. Brian drove himself to school. Mom and Dad took me to the middle school. Everybody stared at us. The hall monitor started to ask us our business but then looked at me and directed us to Mr. Smith's office.

We took seats by his secretary's desk. Miss Lemp was working on some kind of report. She greeted us nervously. At the 8:30 bell, Mr. Smith walked in.

"Good morning. Please come in," he said, nodding at Mom and Dad. We followed him into his office. I sat between Mom and Dad. Mr. Smith sat at his desk and reviewed what had happened the day before. He read a statement from Mr. Pope that told what Tracy had said in his class. He also had an account by the teacher who pulled me into the lockers.

"Mr. McClure was afraid the fight would continue. In the heat of the moment, he overreacted. He feels terrible about what happened," Mr. Smith said.

Mom cleared her throat. "My husband and I understand that what Mr. McClure did was an accident. But it's most upsetting to see our daughter injured because another student picked a fight with her. It's been hard for us to deal with Elaine's death. We don't need to be reminded of it in such an insulting way." She kept her voice low and calm, but a thread of tension ran through it. Her fingers gripped the arms of her chair. I looked at Dad. He sat very still and straight, but the muscles showed along his jaw line.

Mr. Smith cleared his throat. "I remember seeing Elaine a few times when she attended our school. I'm very sorry things turned out as they did," he said gently.

I shouldn't have been surprised. Elaine had to have gotten in trouble at school. But it was odd that Mr. Smith hadn't mentioned that before now.

He took off his glasses and looked directly at me. "I never told you that your sister spent time in my office, Gina. I didn't want you to think that you might be following in her footsteps."

I nodded but couldn't reply.

"Couldn't Mr. Pope have done something to prevent the fight?" asked Dad.

"He didn't know what to do," I answered, surprising myself by doing so. "He couldn't get Tracy to apologize, so he gave her an office detention."

Mom pursed her lips.

"Well," said Mr. Smith, shifting in his seat, "I can arrange for a transfer to another social studies class for Tracy. That will limit her contact with Gina."

Dad nodded, but I said, "No, that's all right. Let her stay in Mr. Pope's class."

"Are you sure?" Mr. Smith asked.

"Yes. There won't be any more problems." I was sure she wouldn't irritate me again. Everybody would know who had given her the shiner.

"Do you know if the other girl is here today?" Dad asked.

Mr. Smith straightened his shoulders. "I won't allow a confrontation," he said firmly.

"That's not why I'm asking. I think Gina needs to apologize to her."

I jerked my head around—too quickly—and stared pop-eyed at Dad. A fraction of a second later, my brain caught up, and I got a pounding headache. "What?!"

Dad turned and looked at me calmly. "You should apologize for hitting her. You can't just hit somebody because she gets on your last nerve. An apology will put an end to it." I knew by the tone of his voice that I would do as he said. I looked at the floor.

"It would be the right thing to do," Mr. Smith said.

The meeting was over. Mom and Dad shook hands with Mr. Smith, and he held the door for us as we left his office. I was surprised to see Tracy and her parents waiting by Miss Lemp's desk.

I had to get it over with, so I walked over to Tracy. She shrank away a little, and her mom and dad bristled like porcupines. "Tracy, I'm really sorry about what happened. I shouldn't have hit you," I said then just stood there like a dummy, staring at her shiner.

The skin around her left eye was bruised purple and red. Her eye was puffy and completely swollen shut. It looked like she had a knothole on her face.

I truly did feel sorry. While I could deal with the way she pestered Greg, I didn't like how she'd talked about Elaine. But hitting her didn't make me proud. I put my hands behind my back.

Her parents relaxed a little. Her mother put her hand gently on Tracy's shoulder.

"I'm sorry, too. It won't happen again," Tracy said. I was sure her parents made her say it, but that was all right. Tracy's father even said how sorry he was about Elaine's death.

Mr. Smith introduced our parents to each other. After speaking briefly, Tracy's parents excused themselves. Mom and Dad thanked Mr. Smith for his time and left for work.

Mr. Smith gestured Tracy and me into his office and spoke to us for a long time about what had happened. I sat in my chair and fidgeted. Whenever I glanced at Tracy, she kept her eyes on him, but her feet kicked out uncontrollably. From there, he took us to the detention room. Mrs. Johnson gave us seats in opposite corners. We heard Mr. Smith call in two hall monitors and instruct them to collect our assignments.

Afterword

IT'S ALREADY THE LAST DAY OF THE SUSPENSION. I'VE LIKED having the quiet time to think about things, but it will be nice to go back to class again. Tracy and I have kept to our corners, and I don't really notice her anymore. Mrs. Johnson has kept a very sharp eye on us, no matter who else has come in for a visit.

I learned that it's stupid to try to keep everything to myself. Mom and Dad said they'd rather hear about my problems. They said that Elaine wouldn't talk to them, and they blamed themselves for not knowing what was on her mind.

I used to be so worried because I looked different from everyone else. So my eyes don't match. So I'm not skinny. Big deal! Life is hard enough without making it worse for myself.

No offense to Mrs. Johnson, but I wouldn't mind not seeing this room again for quite a while. I can't wait to walk out of here and get on with my life.

Writing in this notebook made me take a hard look at some things I never could have told anyone about. Maybe if I hadn't gotten in trouble, I never would have figured out all of this. Brian was right when he said that Elaine didn't give me a chance to know her. Mom was also right when she said that she hadn't finished with Elaine. I guess we weren't finished being sisters, either. It's a great relief to let it go at that. I've been hanging onto the memory of her—or the person I thought she might have been—like a child hangs onto a balloon. It won't be easy, but I'm going to let the balloon go.